Murder

at

Five Oaks

Stables

*

The Lady Jane & Mrs Forbes Mysteries

Book Five

B. D. CHURSTON

This is a work of fiction. All names, characters, locations and incidents are products of the author's imagination or have been used fictitiously. Any resemblance to actual persons living or dead, locales, or events is entirely coincidental. No part of this book may be reproduced without prior written permission from the author.

Copyright © 2025 B. D. CHURSTON

ISBN: 9798282361988

One

Twenty-seven-year-old historian and archaeologist, Lady Jane Scott was at the wheel of her burgundy and black four-seater Triumph Super Seven, driving herself and Aunt Kate along an East Sussex country lane on a sunny Friday afternoon.

"Do you know what, Aunt? After two weeks in a library researching the lavish excesses of Henry the Eighth's court, I'm ready to eat, drink, and be merry!"

"Good for you!" said Kate, laughing at the picture it conjured up for their weekend at Alsop House, a country residence her niece last visited during childhood.

"I bet you can't wait to see Perry," quipped Jane.

Kate glanced at that kindly face and those warm brown eyes – and the mischievous smile. Professor Peregrine

Nash would be spending the weekend at the same destination.

"He might not be there," said Kate, refusing to take the bait. "Something important might have come up at the last minute."

Jane almost spluttered.

"He's one of Oxford University's most experienced professors… except when he's with you. Then he's like an excitable undergraduate. Of course he'll be there!"

Kate smiled at Jane's good-natured exaggeration.

"If you say so."

"He's a top-notch catch, Aunt. Don't you dare let him get away."

"You make him sound like a salmon."

Jane laughed.

"Honestly, you two go together like…"

"Rhubarb crumble and custard?"

"I had a sort of 'magical stream through an enchanted forest' image in mind, but that's much better."

Kate smiled again. Since meeting Perry Nash at Penford Priory six months ago, her view of the future had changed completely. She'd been a widow adapting to living alone. Now she wondered if her story might have a new chapter to look forward to.

"I must say," said Jane, "I can't wait to see the horses."

"Me too," said Kate.

Lady Alsop was hosting a weekend riding competition, which Jane's father, the Earl of Oxley, would usually have attended. He was on business in Edinburgh though, so he'd asked Jane to stand in for him. Jane, in turn, asked Aunt Kate to join her, and mentioned it to Professor Nash, knowing there to be a family connection between him and the Alsops.

Perry then wrote to Kate asking if she would be going.

Kate wrote back saying, "I will, if you will."

It had made her feel both warm and silly. Yes, she was in her mid-fifties, and yes, sixty-year-old Perry was a highly respected Professor of History – but what was life if a little youthful mirth wasn't allowed house room.

"Almost there," said Jane.

The lane had come to an end at a wider road, where a white sign with black lettering pointed right:

Lower Fincham 1 mile.

Jane steered the car accordingly.

"A cup of tea and something sweet, Aunt. That's what we need."

"You read my mind!"

For Kate, it seemed strange that she and Jane had lived very much apart until Linton Hall sixteen months ago, when secrets, lies and murder brought them together. It had been a reminder that true friendships can form regardless of the circumstances.

Before long, Lower Fincham came into view with its grey stone Victorian church, whitewashed cottages with thatched roofs, a few shops, the Royal Oak pub with a couple of men outside, a duck pond, and a village green ready for a spring and summer of cricket. To Kate, it was the essence of the word 'picturesque'.

Just past the pond, Jane pulled over by a cottage where a man was repairing a wooden gate.

"Excuse me," she called across her aunt and through the passenger window. "We're heading for Five Oaks. Is it straight on?"

The man looked up from his work and considered the question.

"Straight on for two hundred yards, then turn right after the barn."

"Thanks!" cried Jane as they sped away again.

"Five Oaks?" queried Kate. "I thought we were going to Alsop House."

"We are! The locals know the estate as Five Oaks."

"Oh right. Well, I can probably guess why."

Jane nodded.

"It was Six Oaks until 1870. That's when Sir Edgar Alsop's grandfather decided on a new staircase."

Just past the barn, they waited for a flock of sheep to do the bidding of a shepherdess and her collie. Once the way was clear, Jane headed up the lane.

A quarter of a mile on, they came to a set of open iron gates hung from ancient stone pillars.

"Five Oaks, Aunt!" declared Jane, barely slowing as she roared through onto a long drive across a parkland expanse. "It's half a mile across and the same again from the front gates to a stream along the rear boundary."

"Impressive."

"Can you date the house?" teased Jane.

Kate looked to Alsop House, which appeared to sit in the exact middle of the estate. It was a large, red brick affair with four chimney stacks – the outer stacks being gable-end chimneys. The size of the windows either side of a portico entrance suggested a dwelling with plenty of large rooms.

"Um… 1750?"

"Ooh, close! It's 1768."

"It's lovely," said Kate.

A hundred yards or so to the right of the building stood the five mighty oaks. Kate was no expert on trees, but their size told her they would have been present for many centuries.

To the left of the house, sat a more recent addition – an impressive block of stables with an arched entrance and clocktower. As they neared, Kate could make out a Rolls-Royce, a Bentley, a Vauxhall, an Austin, and a couple of Vincent horseboxes parked along a fifty-yard track between the stables and the house.

A few moments later, they came to a halt on crunchy gravel by the portico entrance. Almost immediately, the red front door opened and a portly, ageing butler emerged. Once they were out of the car, he greeted them warmly.

"Mrs Forbes, welcome to Alsop House. Lady Jane, welcome back."

Jane beamed. "Mr Brooke, you haven't changed a bit!"

"Now, now, Lady Jane, I think we can both see I'm older and wider. You've certainly changed though. I hope it's not out of place to say you've grown up wonderfully!"

"You're too kind, Mr Brooke."

Just then, a keen young footman hurried past the butler and approached the car.

"This is Richards," said Brooke. "He'll take your bags to your rooms and move your vehicle to the parking area. If you'd care to follow me, I'll let Lady Alsop know you've arrived."

Two

Kate and Jane stepped into a vestibule the size of a small ballroom. With an upper floor gallery facing them and the 1870 L-shaped oak staircase sweeping down from it on the left-hand side, the grand entrance at Alsop House had clearly been designed to impress.

The staircase itself descended against the wall to a halfway landing, from where it turned to come down a quarter of the way into the vestibule. Facing the stairs, across a scuffed black and white chessboard tiled floor, a huge, ancient stone fireplace added to the intended grandeur.

As for the rest of the vestibule, the walls hosted a few dour Victorian portraits in oil, while the high ceiling featured ornate but cracked plasterwork and a droplet chandelier that had seen better days – all of which accentuated the modernity of the shiny black telephone on a side table.

Having handed their jackets to Brooke, Kate enjoyed the freedom of being down to a lilac two-piece and a thin grey cardigan, while Jane looked vibrant in a light green day dress.

Brooke meanwhile glanced upward.

"Ah, that saves me a journey."

Lady Alsop had appeared at the top of the stairs, descending calmly. This widow in her fifties had an elegant, upright gait and looked well in a purple ankle-length dropped waist dress. Oddly, an angular woman of a similar age trailed behind, speaking in hushed tones.

"You *must*, Imelda."

"Not now, my dear," insisted Lady Alsop.

"If you won't call the police, I will."

"Just leave it with me."

Kate felt that she and Jane should go out and come in again. As it was, at the halfway turn, the whispering ladies spotted the fresh arrivals and fell conspicuously silent, leaving Kate to smile awkwardly up at them.

The angular woman nodded and returned up the stairs, leaving Lady Alsop to descend the rest of the way alone.

"Mrs Forbes and Lady Jane, Ma'am," Brooke informed her.

"Thank you, Brooke. That will be all."

As Brooke went off with the jackets, Lady Alsop eyed Richards coming in with the first wave of bags.

"Take those straight up to our guests' rooms."

"Yes, Ma'am."

With young Richards climbing the stairs, Lady Alsop addressed her guests.

"Mrs Forbes, Jane… welcome to Alsop House."

"Lady Alsop, it's lovely to see you again after all these years," said Jane.

"Likewise, my dear. And you must both call me Imelda. I'm not one for formalities under my own roof."

Kate smiled. "We'll be friends in no time if you call me Kate."

"Kate…" echoed Imelda warmly.

"I must say, you have a lovely home, Imelda. It's so full of character."

"Thank you. Jane knows it well, of course. I'm sure she'll show you around."

"Absolutely," said Jane. "It's been a while, though. I might suggest the drawing room and wander into the kitchen by mistake."

"All the more fun," said Imelda. "And Jane, as a student of history, you might appreciate the fact you'll be the first woman to present the Alsop Challenge Cup."

"I'm looking forward to it."

Imelda turned to Kate.

"Dear Edgar presented the trophy for twenty-five years, then Robert kindly took over. Of course, for many years, Edgar was a competitor too, which meant I couldn't allow him to win, even when he was the best in the field. Well, I could hardly have him presenting the trophy to himself."

"Diplomacy at its finest," observed Kate.

"It's by no means a big competition but it's a much loved one."

"I'm sure my father won it when he was second best to Sir Edgar," said Jane.

"Your mother, bless her, loved watching your father compete."

"Yes…" said Jane, lowering her gaze.

Kate smiled sadly. It wasn't far off the tenth anniversary of Spanish flu taking Jane's mother, Annette, from them. Annette had been Kate's younger sister. Despite the sadness of the memory, it constantly bolstered Kate's wish to help Jane in every way possible.

"But what of you, Jane?" said Lady Alsop. "Have you met anyone yet?"

Jane gave a coy smile.

"There's a chap called Harry."

"You must tell me all about him later. Perhaps he'll show you how life doesn't have to be all dusty documents and muddy pits."

"Possibly not – he's a fellow historian and archaeologist."

"Ah, that could work very well indeed. I do hope you're happy, Jane."

"I am, thanks."

"Um…" ventured Kate, "I understand your second cousin might be coming down from Oxford."

"Perry? Yes, he arrived an hour ago. He's in the library looking at lots of old books. Do you know him?"

"Yes, we're on good terms."

"Perry's mother and mine were great friends," said Lady Alsop. "Perry and I know each other a lot less though. I was a little surprised to hear from him but pleased too. He seems a good sort."

Kate smiled.

"He is."

"Now, would you like to see your rooms?" said Lady Alsop. "I'm sure you'll want to rest after your journey."

This comment seemed more aimed at Kate than her perky niece.

"That would be lovely," said the former.

As if by magic, a young maid appeared.

"Connie will take you up," said Lady Alsop. "And as you don't appear to travel with a maid, she'll be at your service for anything you need."

Connie half-curtsied and headed for the stairs.

Kate and Jane followed.

It was a lovely house, although the carpet runner seemed a little worn, while a large ornamental vase on the landing at the top of the stairs appeared to be of low quality. Still, Kate wasn't there to judge. She was simply thankful to be a guest and would show her gratitude to Lady Alsop in any way she could.

Three

Connie was unpacking Kate's things into a small, rickety wardrobe and an old chest of drawers – chatting as she did so.

"Everyone's looking forward to tomorrow... it's so exciting... I've no idea who'll win, mind... as for now, if you stroll around the grounds... Mr Russell keeps the grass in order... you'll see pots of daffs, primroses and crocuses here and there on the terrace... he's not here though... visiting a sick sister... Rosie... got trouble with her knee..."

"Connie, may I ask... Lady Alsop was with another woman when we arrived. A thin lady of a similar age."

"That's Mrs Glessing. They've known each other for ages. Since they were girls, I think."

"I see."

Connie's activity came to a halt. Her task was done.

"If that's all, Mrs Forbes, I'll help Lady Jane."

"Thank you, Connie."

The maid opened the door to reveal the butler arriving with a tray of tea and shortbread biscuits for two.

"Will you and Lady Jane take tea together?" he asked as he replaced Connie in the doorway. "Or shall I divide the spoils?"

"Thank you, Mr Brooke. Put the tray on the table; we'll take tea in here."

"Very good, Madam."

Once the butler had departed, Kate turned to a wall mirror to check her collar-length hair. Yes, the forces of grey were thriving amid her dark brown locks, but her dedication to regular walking meant the rest of her was in pretty good shape for her age.

She sat down on the edge of the bed and studied the sunlit, white-washed room. The tiled fireplace would no doubt be called into service come the morning, while a small red rug and a soft, faded floral armchair added a touch of homely comfort. To Kate, it was easily possible to sense a certain 'tiredness' in Alsop House, although – countering this – there was the modern marvel of electric lights.

There was also a spectacular view of the grounds to the rear of the house, a large part of which would make up the competition course on Saturday afternoon.

Kate supposed Jane would have quite fancied a ride herself. She was good on horseback over open country, but competitive events were the preserve of gentlemen and the military – whether that be at Alsop House or the Olympic Games.

There was a knock at the door.

"Come in."

Jane entered with a smile.

"Connie's putting my things away."

"She has a lovely manner and she's very helpful. It must be tempting for you to travel with a maid of your own."

"Apart from a maid in London, I prefer to look after myself, Aunt."

"Jane, you're the daughter of an earl."

"Yes, but not an overly pampered one."

"Well, if that's the case, you can pour the tea."

Jane happily did so.

"These rooms have a lovely view, don't they, Aunt. The grounds are just as I remember – perfect for horse riding."

"It looks perfect for a good stroll, too."

Jane handed her aunt a cup of tea.

"Aunt Kate…? What do you think of that woman's mention of the police?"

"You mean Mrs Glessing? She's an old friend of Lady Alsop's."

"My, you've been busy."

"I'm sure it's nothing, Jane. At least, it's none of our business."

"As usual, you're right."

"It's good for Imelda to have a friend at hand. She must miss her husband."

"I'm sure she does."

A moment of reflection passed.

Then Jane's eyes lit up.

"I bet you can't wait to see Perry."

Kate baulked at the suddenness of the comment.

"I'm not eighteen."

"So?" said Jane with a cheeky smile.

"Well… yes, alright, I'm looking forward to seeing him. It's a pity we live so far apart."

"You'll sort it out. I know it."

There was no denying it. Things weren't ideal. Apart from getting together a few times, the six months since they first met had been conducted mainly through weekly letters and telephone calls. She felt blessed to have met Perry Nash, but they needed to find a more suitable way forward. However, loud voices from below brought any further thoughts on the matter to a halt.

"Someone sounds agitated," said Jane.

With the sash window open a little, they listened as they peered down at a lean man in his fifties arguing with a younger man on the terrace. It seemed to revolve around the younger man's refusal to go along with something.

A moment later, the older man returned to the house, leaving the younger one to throw his hands up in frustration.

Kate studied him – tall, lithe, long-ish blond hair, wearing plus fours and a gaudy knitted green jumper. She wondered if he might be a hellraiser.

"I'm sure that's Jasper Evans," said Jane. "I last saw him when I was ten or eleven. That would make the older man his father, Dr Evans. He did look familiar."

"I expect we'll get to meet them soon enough," said Kate. "Right now though, let's finish our tea and do some exploring."

"Good idea, Aunt. Where shall we start? The grounds? The stables…?"

"I thought the library."

Jane laughed.

"The library it is."

Four

The stairs brought them down to the huge vestibule.

"Which way, Jane?"

"Let me see if I can get my bearings…" Jane went to the front door and turned. "Just trying to recreate it from memory."

She pointed ahead where, beneath the gallery, there were two doors.

"Drawing room on the right, sitting room on the left."

She walked towards them, passing Kate, who joined her.

Now Jane looked right into a hallway. "That leads to the morning room, dining room, kitchen and staff areas."

She turned and headed for the other hallway.

"This gives us Sir Edgar's study and the music room facing onto the front of the house… and the library and billiards room facing the terrace."

The first door on the right was open.

"Voila," announced Jane.

Thanks to French doors and a sash window facing onto the terrace and grounds to the rear of the house, the sizeable library was bright. Indeed, the sunlight streaming through the glass captured the dust motes resulting from many old books being recently disturbed. There was no shortage of tomes either. Apart from one section of wall that displayed a framed painting of an old stone bridge over a stream, most of the room was turned over to bookcases crammed to overflowing.

For Kate, this just left the business of what to say to the man from Oxford University.

Obviously, 'hello' was a candidate.

Perry was standing by one of the bookcases on the far side. Grey hair. A soft cotton shirt under a brown pullover. He'd just removed a book from the shelf and blown forcefully along its top edge to release yet more dust into the room.

Regardless of that, Kate was pleased to see him. In fact, this would become a mission to find the right moment to ask how serious he was about them being together. And it would start right away, with some friendly words to soften him up.

"With you here, I know it's going to be a lovely weekend," she said.

"You're too kind," said a woman at a bookcase behind the door.

"Ah…" said Kate while both Perry and Jane had to stifle their laughter.

"How lovely to see you both," said Perry. "This is Mrs Glessing, a friend of Imelda's. Mrs Glessing, this is Mrs Kate Forbes and her niece, Lady Jane Scott."

"Lovely to meet you," said Kate to the woman who had attempted to counsel Lady Alsop on the staircase earlier.

"Hello, Mrs Glessing," said Jane. "I visited Alsop House a few times when I was much younger. I don't know if you remember me."

"Yes, I remember you well. What fun we had back then."

Kate gave up hope of hearing Mrs Glessing's first name.

"Did you have a good journey?" asked Perry.

"We did," said Kate. "And yourself?"

"Yes – a fast train to London then a slower one down to Eastbourne, where I got a taxi."

Mrs Glessing smiled indulgently.

"I'm giving the professor some pointers on evaluating the library's contents," she said.

"Evaluating?" uttered Kate.

"It's why I'm here," said Perry, his eyes imploring her to cotton on to his false excuse for being at Alsop House.

"Ah… yes… Jane mentioned you possibly being here this weekend… sorting out the library."

"Are you here mainly for the horses?" Mrs Glessing asked Kate.

"Yes, the Alsop Cup sounds exciting."

"The Alsop *Challenge* Cup," said Mrs Glessing, correcting her. Her eyes then narrowed. "Do you know the professor?"

Not well enough… "Yes, a little."

Jane smirked.

"Obviously, it's a happy coincidence that the professor is visiting his second cousin, Lady Alsop, for the first time since he was sixteen."

Kate smiled at Perry and felt an urge to give him a hug, but Mrs Glessing's steady gaze put her off.

"I know it's none of my business," said Kate, "but was everything all right with Lady Alsop earlier?" Kate ignored Jane's raised eyebrow. "You seemed concerned for her."

"Everything is *not* all right, Mrs Forbes, but as you've suggested, it's a private matter."

"Of course. My apologies. Well, Perry, you appear to have a mountain of books to get through."

"According to Mrs Glessing, it's *two* mountains."

"There's an overspill room," explained Mrs Glessing. "Imelda hasn't thrown out anything of Sir Edgar's."

"I'll be here till Christmas," said Perry, picking up another book and blowing across the top.

"You may as well see it all first, Professor," said Mrs Glessing before turning to Kate. "Professor Nash and I will leave you here. It's very cramped up there. We'd spend the whole time bumping into each other."

Kate stepped back to make way as Mrs Glessing swept out of the room with Perry in tow.

"Aunt? I thought you said Imelda's police matter was none of our business."

"Yes, well…. did you have fun with Mrs Glessing when you were a child?"

"No, she saw children as a nuisance."

"I thought so. But let's not judge. None of us know other people's stories unless they choose to reveal them. I'm sure Mrs Glessing isn't all bad. In fact… how about we start getting to know her better?"

"You mean follow her up to the overspill room."

A few moments later, at the top of the stairs, aunt and niece paused by the ugly vase.

"Which way?" wondered Kate.

They found the room at the end of the men's wing. It was much bigger than suggested – the space limitation having more to do with the volume of junk filling it.

Books were stuffed into two old bookcases and piled high on the floor across one side of the room. There were also various figurines and Royal commemoration cups on a shelf – none of great value. Elsewhere, there was a wonky wardrobe, a broken occasional chair, a broken vase, a pile of magazines, and a large country style wicker storage trunk.

"You shouldn't have bothered," said Mrs Glessing. "The room is full of dust because nobody is allowed in here. Now there'll be four of us disturbing it."

"Only another two thousand books here," said Perry without much joy.

Jane lifted the hinged wicker lid of the trunk and peered inside.

"Clothes," she muttered, closing the lid again.

Kate picked up a small but beautiful lamp. The shade fell off the mounting.

"Edgar brought that back from Paris in 1910 or so," said Mrs Glessing.

Perry picked up a couple of books, glanced at the spines, shook his head, and placed them on the trunk.

Kate wondered. Had a temporary storage room evolved into a permanent fixture? Or would Perry Nash genuinely make inroads into this lot?

She glanced at the books he'd put down.

"The Empress of Watering Places," she said, reading the uppermost volume. "A Brief History of Eastbourne's Seaside, 1752 – 1920."

"You could write one of those for Sandham-on-Sea," said Jane as she opened a cabinet – which was chock full of more books.

Perry sighed.

"It's all so… fascinating."

To Kate, the look on his face was saying 'Help!'

"Perhaps the library is enough for now," she suggested.

"Agreed," said Perry, heading for the door.

Five

With the back of Alsop House facing south-west, the terrace enjoyed any sunshine from lunchtime until sunset, which made it perfect for summertime get-togethers. On an afternoon in March, the weather was wonderful, but perhaps the evenings would be too chilly to be outside.

From the grounds at the rear, Kate and Jane admired the majestic five oaks. As for the house, bathed in sunshine, that was looking rather grand too.

From their standpoint, its left-hand end housed a huge kitchen. Then came four large rooms: the dining room, drawing room, sitting room and library – each originally having two large sash windows. However, the alterations of 1905 replaced a sash window in each of the four rooms with a set of French doors. The idea was to have the ground floor flow out onto the terrace to enhance those summertime soirees. The billiards room was last on the right. This lacked French doors though.

The sash windows of the floor above were those of the rear-facing bedrooms. Above this line came the attic dormer windows of the staff bedrooms.

To the right of the house there was the fifty-yard gap to the stables block with its arched entrance and clock tower, from where a chestnut horse and its rider emerged to address the competition course. This took man and beast beyond the stables and out towards the woods, where they covered a hundred yards before turning right towards the rear of the estate. Reaching a yellow flag on a pole just short of the stream, they turned again and raced back to the finish line. Half a mile in all, over five low fences built for spectacle more than difficulty. The real challenge was to beat the clock.

"Lady Jane!"

Kate and Jane turned to an earnest-looking young man with rounded features. He was waving as he approached.

"A friend, Jane?" asked Kate.

"Possibly."

"David Marston," he announced as he drew near, his diamond tie clip dazzling Kate. "You must remember me?"

"David, of course. How are you?"

"All the better for seeing you, Jane. When I heard you'd arrived, I couldn't wait to say hello. How you've grown! And not married, I hear?"

"No, I'm not married. How about you?"

"Just waiting for the right woman to come along."

He was eyeing Jane like a slice of chocolate cake.

"David, let me introduce my aunt, Mrs Kate Forbes."

The introductions quickly revealed David Marston to have been a childhood visitor to Alsop House, and his and Jane's paths crossing a few times. He was now a junior manager at a paint retailer in Eastbourne with *significant* prospects.

"Are your parents here?" asked Jane.

"Oh, they don't come anymore. It's up to me to keep the Marston flag flying these days. Now, how about a little excitement? I'm running a sweepstake to add some spice to the competition. Ten bob apiece. I've sold five of the eight tickets so far."

Kate didn't think much of Mr Marston. A little flutter on the horses though...

"I'll take one," she said.

"Me too," said Jane.

"Wonderful! Once I've sold the last ticket, I'll put the horses' names in a hat, and we'll have a grand draw. Winner takes all."

"They look a good pairing," said Kate, indicating the horse and rider they had been watching. The rider, much nearer now, was possibly in his early thirties.

Marston followed her gaze.

"Ah, Lady Alsop's godson, Mr Deerhurst on Nero. The horse only arrived an hour ago. Just needs to settle in."

"*Jonathan* Deerhurst?" asked Jane.

"Yes, I expect you remember him."

Jane turned to her aunt.

"Jonathan was older than us by three or four years, so he hated to spend time playing children's games. He tended to stick with the adults as much as possible."

Just then, a rider wearing an army tunic went out from the stables. David Marston pointed to him.

"Major Peter Tipton of the 11th Hussars on Apollo."

"The cavalry," said Jane.

To Kate, Major Tipton had a confident manner. Imperious, even. With thinning, oily dark grey hair and a neat grey moustache, he looked to be in his mid-fifties.

"I remember him," said Jane. "He spent most of his time with Sir Edgar."

"That's right," said Marston. "He was a captain back then. That's his valet." He was indicating a chap in his forties emerging from the stables. "Former Lance Corporal Stamford. He was Tipton's batman during the War."

As it was, Major Tipton and Apollo performed admirably – effortlessly gliding over the first fence. Kate could see they were a good pairing.

"I'd say the major has a fair chance," she said.

"Yes, he's been here since Wednesday, so he'll know the course better than anyone."

"A regular visitor then."

"Very much so. He helped Lady Alsop when Sir Edgar died. Far be it from me to chinwag, but some say he has his eye on her."

"Ah, the curse of gossip," said Kate, watching Appollo take the next fence with ease.

"Absolutely, Mrs Forbes. I hate gossip. That said, some say he has a rival."

"Will there be more competitors arriving in the morning?" asked Kate by way of changing the subject.

"Yes, a few who don't have to travel far."

"Do they bring their own horses?" asked Jane.

"Yes – the only riders borrowing a horse from Lady Alsop are myself and Jasper Evans. Not that we're able to choose from a vast string. She only has four in the stables."

Kate thought the stables looked too big for such a small number.

"Well, I'll leave you to it," said Marston, his eyes flashing at the younger of the ladies.

As he headed back to the house, Kate puffed out her cheeks.

"I think you have an admirer, Jane."

Six

A short while later, the two riders brought their mounts to a slow walk alongside each other, not far from the ladies. Indeed, a friendly argument broke out between them. In Kate's opinion, the cavalry man, Major Tipton, seemed to be teasing Mr Deerhurst for the benefit of the onlookers.

"I won't have it, Deerhurst. A civilian competing on horseback wouldn't have been allowed in the old days."

Deerhurst laughed amiably.

"You should report it to the Olympic committee, Major Tipton."

"Olympic committee, my foot!"

"It's they who changed the rules – not me."

"Indeed, it's a rum do. At least do me the courtesy of letting me win."

"What! A former cavalry major hardly needs fear an amateur!"

Tipton dismounted with a smile and handed the horse to his valet. Deerhurst handed his to a stable boy.

"Is it Lady Jane from all those years ago?" asked Deerhurst.

"It is, and it's good to see you, Jonathan."

"You too, dear Jane."

"Ladies," said Tipton by way of a greeting.

He too recalled Jane from the old days, which just left the matter of Jane introducing Aunt Kate.

Tipton then asked after Jane's father and revealed that he knew she would be standing in as presenter of the trophy – to which he added:

"I look forward to accepting it from you tomorrow."

He followed this with a wink, which assured Kate that he was human after all.

"Have you come far?" asked Jane.

"I live in Eastbourne now that I've retired from army life. Deerhurst here is down from London."

"Me too," said Jane.

Kate wondered. Did the major really have his eye on Lady Alsop? Not that it was any of her business, of course.

The men soon made their excuses and headed back to the house while the horses were led to the stables.

One thing that stood out was Major Tipton throwing a comment to a confident-looking man on the terrace, perhaps in his fifties. He was dressed in a dark blue suit and wore metal-framed glasses.

"When are you returning to London, Hammond?"

"Monday or Tuesday, old boy. Not trying to get rid of me, are you?"

A moment later, Hammond approached the ladies.

"Archie Hammond at your service."

The introductions revealed Archibald Hammond to be a cousin on Sir Edgar's side of the family.

"I recall you," said Jane. "I came here a few times with my parents before the War. You were always cheery."

"Ah, the good old days! I was a regular visitor back then. I trust I haven't changed, Lady Jane."

"I'm sure you haven't."

He glanced at Tipton.

"A fine chap," he declared.

"Major Tipton?" asked Kate.

"Yes, he has Lady Alsop's interests very much at heart."

Kate wasn't sure what to make of the comment.

"We're here for the competition, Mr Hammond. We're very much looking forward to it."

"Me too, Mrs Forbes. I wouldn't miss it for the world."

"Will you be riding?" asked Kate.

"Oh, I'm no rider. I've worked tirelessly to achieve a senior position in the City of London. Even today, supposedly enjoying myself, I'm reading detailed contracts." He patted his jacket pocket. "I won't risk a broken neck falling off a horse."

"Quite so," said Kate. "Not everyone is confident around horses."

"Do you know anyone here, Mrs Forbes?"

"Well…"

"I thought I heard mention of a friendship with Professor Nash…?"

"Ah… yes, we're friends. He's here to go through the contents of Lady Alsop's library."

"Yes, Mrs Glessing mentioned Imelda having no appetite for disposing of Edgar's things – until now, seemingly. If the professor comes across any valuable books, I could help sell them. I think the money would be welcomed."

With that, he wished them well and headed back to the house.

"Jane!" The raised voice belonged to an attractive young woman in her mid-twenties dressed in a canary yellow creation.

"Eliza!" exclaimed Jane. "What a lovely surprise!"

Kate learned that Miss Eliza Cole was a regular visitor to Alsop House and that her late mother had been a friend of Lady Alsop. She also learned that Jane had been a year above Eliza at school.

"Aunt Kate's fussing over me for the next few days," explained Jane.

"How wonderful to have such attention," said Eliza.

"I'm sure we have lots to talk about," said Jane.

"We do – and I've lots of news to share. It's top secret for the moment though, so I can't say a word for now."

"Exciting," said Jane.

"Eliza… there you are."

It was a woman, possibly in her late thirties, wearing a light grey twinset and flat brown shoes.

"I must go," said Eliza. "I've promised Miss Pearce some advice on the latest fashions. She won't follow them. It's the thrill of the prospect, I think. It gets her heart racing!"

Eliza duly hurried off to join Miss Pearce.

"Eliza's a pleasant young woman," said Kate.

"Yes, she is. It must be the first time I've seen her since… oh, a party in London a couple of years ago."

"She lost her mother…?"

"Yes, the rest of her family lives in South Africa. She was sent to England for school and never went back. Last I heard, she was living with an elderly aunt. I wasn't expecting to see her here though. I'll have to find out more."

"Well, it's tea and cake soon, Jane. How about a little stroll to justify the intake?"

Seven

Following their stroll, Kate and Jane returned to the dining room where Connie was on hand to serve tea and cake. This was an informal affair with the French doors onto the terrace open meaning that guests took what they wanted and generally milled around engaging in chatter, both inside and outside the house.

However, before Kate could get to the table, Mrs Glessing entered from the hallway.

"Ah, Mrs Glessing…" Kate had one eye on the woman in question, the other on a slice of chocolate cake. "How are things in the library?"

"Professor Nash is doing a fine job. Oh, it's good to meet a man who's married to his work. I find it ever so stimulating."

Kate didn't like the sound of that.

"Will he be joining us?"

"Yes, he'll be along shortly. To be frank, I couldn't fathom why he would come down from Oxford to go through all those dusty books. He's sneezed at least a dozen times. But I'm glad he has. I feel we have a mutual understanding."

"Oh…" was all Kate could muster.

"You probably haven't noticed, Mrs Forbes, but he's jolly good company."

"Is that so."

Jonathan Deerhurst nodded to them from the terrace as he passed by the open doors. Once he was out of earshot, Mrs Glessing lowered her voice.

"Jane? Mr Deerhurst is an intriguing chap, don't you think?"

"We saw him riding Nero," said Kate, changing the emphasis. "What a handsome beast."

"Yes, and he has money too."

"I was referring to the horse," said Kate.

"Ah… a good steed. I don't suppose you know many of Imelda's guests?"

"As you know, I'm here to accompany Jane, but it seems a very friendly gathering."

"Oh, it is."

Kate glanced out at Mr Deerhurst who was now with a woman they had seen earlier.

"That's Miss Sophie Pearce," said Mrs Glessing. "His private secretary. I know almost nothing about her, but I understand she's new. Now… have I told you about my grandfather?"

Kate feigned deafness and headed for the table, where she was beaten to the chocolate cake by the swift arrival of David Marston. She hoped it wasn't a punishment for abandoning Mrs Glessing.

As it was, Marston became absorbed in cutting the thinnest slice possible from the body of the cake – which led Kate to wonder if he might be on a diet.

"It's for Lady Alsop," he explained. "I know exactly how thin she likes it."

Kate smiled. *Thin? It's practically see-through.*

"Same for you, Aunt?" said a mischievous Jane as she waited to take the cake knife from Marston.

"Just a little less thin for me, Jane." Kate held up a thumb and forefinger separated by an inch.

"Lady Alsop is looking ever so well," said Marston, placing the meagre slice on a plate and handing the knife to Jane. "She looks younger with each passing year."

He left by the French doors, with Mrs Glessing following him. A moment later, Kate got to sink her teeth into the slice of cake Jane had just passed to her.

With her mouth full, Perry Nash came in.

"Ah, there you are, ladies."

His face broke into a warm smile which had to linger until Kate could swallow.

"Are you still sneezing your way through the afternoon," she finally said.

"Oh, it's not so bad. I'm used to a little dust. What I'm not used to is a forest of mediocre books that nobody seems to care about."

"Think of the greater objective," said Jane. "You're here with Aunt Kate."

"Yes, of course." He smiled again. "What about you two? Have you settled in?"

"Completely," said Jane. "We watched a couple of the riders out practicing earlier."

"And we've entered a sweepstake for the competition," said Kate. "That said, Imelda doesn't have many horses of her own. I wonder if there's a commitment to keeping the stables going."

"Oh," said Perry. "I suppose something Antonia said might offer a clue – Imelda was a leisure rider up until recently, when she lost her pet horse."

Kate frowned.

"Who's Antonia?"

"Antonia Glessing. You met her earlier, Kate."

"Ah, yes."

That woman moves faster than any of the horses!

"According to Antonia, the competition began as a bet in 1880 – not that she approves of gambling. Apparently, they had twenty competitors back then. Now it's eight."

"A shadow of its former self then," observed Jane.

David Marston appeared at the French doors.

"I have one more sweepstake ticket left to sell. Professor?"

"Mrs Glessing says gambling never pays," Perry informed him.

Marston grinned. "Mrs Glessing has strong views on most things. Are you sure I can't persuade you?"

"Go on then," said Perry. "Who knows, it might be the lucky ticket."

Once the transaction had been completed, Marston declared that the draw would take place in a few minutes on the terrace.

Although they followed him outside, Kate lured Perry aside, and then farther along the terrace towards the library.

"The draw's taking place over there, Kate," he said, pointing the other way.

"I just wanted to say how much I enjoy our correspondence," she told him.

"Me too."

"I just think we don't see each other often enough – including here at Alsop House, it would seem."

Perry smiled. "I feel the same way."

"You really mean that?"

"Yes, absolutely."

"Then perhaps we should do something about it."

"I agree, but I'm tied to Oxford, and you're tied to Sandham."

"Yes… that's true."

"I'm sure we'll work something out, Kate. In the meantime, I have Antonia to deal with."

Kate smiled but then became solemn.

"Did she say anything about a problem Imelda's dealing with?"

"No…?"

"It's just that when Jane and I first arrived, she was advising her to call the police."

"Oh… is that the private matter you mentioned in the library?"

"Yes."

Perry shrugged.

"Sorry, no idea, Kate."

"Well… Mr Marston's sweepstake then."

On route to joining the small crowd, Kate glanced through the sitting room sash window. Major Tipton was inside with Eliza Cole. It wasn't possible to hear what they were discussing, and there was no way to remain there without appearing to be nosy, which Kate wished to avoid.

Eight

All were soon gathered on the sunny terrace where David Marston was brandishing a ladies' hat which held eight pieces of card.

"Without further ado, let's see who has what for tomorrow afternoon's Alsop Challenge Cup. Simply take a card to discover your horse. Lady Alsop…?"

Lady Alsop took a dip and read the card.

"Misty."

"Jasper's on Misty," Marston pointed out.

Lady Alsop's response was non-committal. Not that Jasper would have known. He was nowhere to be seen.

Jane was second to pull a card from the hat.

"Horatio."

"I'm on Horatio!" cried Marston. He would have clapped his hands together had he not been holding the hat.

"Wonderful," said Jane, giving nothing away.

"I know you'll cheer me on wildly!" enthused Marston.

Kate was next.

"Nero… Mr Deerhurst's horse, which I think gives me a real chance."

She and the rider exchanged conspiratorial grins.

Next came Perry, Dr Evans, Archie Hammond, and Eliza Cole – all of whom drew a horse and rider that wouldn't be arriving until the morning.

"And finally, the staff ticket," announced Marston.

Connie the maid stepped forward self-consciously but received much encouragement as she drew the final card.

"Apollo," she declared before turning to Brooke the butler, who smiled warmly.

Jane leaned into Kate's ear.

"Sir Edgar always paid for a staff ticket, so that everyone could enjoy the big day. Imelda has continued it."

A free ticket for the staff? And a decent pot of winnings if their horse proved to be the best? Kate approved. In fact, she hoped Major Tipton would ride Apollo to victory.

"May I wish you all the best of luck," declared Marston, who placed the ladies' hat on his head with aplomb.

"Thank you for organizing that, David," said Lady Alsop. "As always, I hope our wonderful members of staff are successful."

Applause broke out, which had Connie looking even more self-conscious before Brooke called her away, possibly to remind her that there were duties to perform.

With the draw over, Kate stepped away towards Perry, who was with Major Tipton. Waiting for her moment, she looked to Imelda, who was suddenly in quiet conversation with Eliza Cole. Indeed, the closer Kate got, the more private it seemed.

Eliza was urging Imelda, "Perhaps delay a little longer… give it some more thought…"

On hearing Imelda's response, "my investments are *my* business", Kate turned away and bumped into Archie Hammond.

"Mr Hammond, I do beg your pardon."

"No harm done, Mrs Forbes. Are you enjoying yourself?"

"Yes, I am, thanks," said Kate, relaxing a little. "Who knows, I might win the sweepstake. I drew Mr Deerhurst on Nero."

"I'm sure he's an excellent competitor."

"He is!" an exuberant Dr Evans extolled as he joined them. "I only arrived after lunch. I had patients to see this morning. Then I had to take my wife to the station. She's off seeing her sister in Lambeth. She's not one for horses."

"Unlike yourself, Doctor?"

"I couldn't wait to get here!"

"It's clearly a much-loved competition," observed Kate. "It seems a few have taken time off work to be here."

"Oh, it's not to be missed. Mind you, I don't have to come far, and it's been easier to get here since a fellow doctor and I joined forces to buy a second-hand Austin."

"Where are you based?" asked Jane.

"A couple of miles away in Eastbourne, not far from the seafront. There's nothing better than a stroll along the promenade or a dip in the sea. Do you know Eastbourne?"

"I do," said Jane.

"Alas, no," said Kate.

"I've not had the pleasure," said Hammond, "but it sounds well worth a visit."

"Oh, it is – and I think I heard Mrs Forbes is a fellow seaside dweller? Is that right?"

"Yes," Kate happily confirmed. "Sandham-on-Sea. A friendly town with a glorious harbour, a lovely beach, and every amenity. Apologies if I sound like I'm drumming up business."

Just then, Eliza came by, which meant that Lady Alsop was free – a situation Hammond seized on.

"If you'll excuse me…"

Kate watched him go, but saw that Eliza was now at a loose end.

"Right, well… I must find my son," said the doctor. "Please do excuse me."

This left Kate and Jane free to join Eliza.

"Well, Jane," said Eliza, "I see you drew David Marston and Horatio in the sweepstake."

"You don't think he fixed the draw, do you?" said Kate.

Jane sighed. "Aunt Kate, you're meant to be the senior figure among us."

Both Jane and Kate broke into a smile.

"You two get on really well," observed Eliza. "It's such a lovely thing to see."

"It's true," said Jane. "We're best friends."

Kate's heart swelled. She only wanted to be the best aunt possible to Jane, and perhaps she wasn't doing a bad job.

"You're so lucky," said Eliza.

"Oh, it comes with responsibility," said Jane in a mock-solemn manner. "For example, Aunt Kate has a very good friendship with Professor Nash which I constantly advise her on. When I say *advise*, I mean egg on."

"I *am* here," Kate pointed out.

"Yes, you are, Aunt, but there comes a time in a woman's life…"

"Jane, that's advice I should be giving you."

Eliza laughed. "I think it's wonderful to have an experienced romantic give advice on affairs of the heart."

Kate smiled. "But you're not sure which of us is the experienced romantic…?"

"No comment," said Eliza.

All three laughed and Kate felt more than ever that this would be a wonderful weekend.

"Last I heard, Eliza," said Jane, "you were living with an aunt. Is she an acquaintance of Lady Alsop?"

"Ah… she was. Aunt Esme passed away in January."

"Oh, I'm so sorry."

Kate added her own sympathies and left a suitable pause before moving the conversation on.

"Do you ride, Eliza?"

"Yes, I ride Ariadne when I'm here. She's one of Lady Alsop's mares with a liking for a steady canter. I'll be going out soon. It should be quiet without the competitors charging about. What about you, Jane? Do you still ride?"

"A little. I enjoy speed though, which worries my father."

"He's not the only one," said Kate. "The speed isn't the problem, it's coming to a sudden, unplanned halt. That's why I don't ride – at any speed."

"I hear you've solved murders," said Eliza. "Any kind of horse-riding must seem tame by comparison."

"Well…" began Kate.

"I'm teasing and I'm sorry," said Eliza. "I don't mean to make light of serious matters. Let's catch up properly later."

Eliza made her excuses and went off to talk with David Marston.

"Look at that," whispered Mrs Glessing as she joined Kate and Jane. "Jasper's not happy."

Jasper had come outside with his father but seemed to be distracted by Eliza talking with Marston.

Mrs Glessing continued. "Jasper and Eliza were together, but I believe it might have come to an end."

"I'm sure they know what's best for them," said Kate.

While Mrs Glessing nattered on, Kate watched Jonathan Deerhurst, who was announcing an intention to check a couple of jumps. Apparently, he wasn't happy with the landing areas. Miss Pearce took that opportunity to tell him that she'd be busy with paperwork in the drawing room but needed to see him about a matter when convenient.

Kate's gaze then returned to Mrs Glessing – mainly because the latter had finally finished speaking.

Kate used the pause to depart and round up Jane and Perry for a stroll.

It was a good ten minutes before they returned to the library where Archie Hammond was sitting reading some paperwork, the sunlight glinting off his glasses.

He got up immediately, folding his papers into his pocket.

"Thought I'd give you a hand, Professor. See if we can find anything of worth." He glanced at the bookcase nearest the door. "Now there's a book. Wilkie Collins, *The Moonstone*."

"Er, yes…" Perry smiled stoically. "Essentially, I'm sorting out what to keep, what to sell, and what to give away to local libraries and schools. Any help would be very welcome. As would helping me to move the table."

"Righto."

Hammond helped him pull the table over to the nearest bookcase where Perry placed some volumes on it. He then turned to Kate and Jane.

"You can help too, if you like. The more the merrier."

Kate sneezed at the dust.

No thanks.

But she thought again. Libraries, books, research – this was the world of Professor Peregrine Nash. She gazed at him, a weighty hardback in each hand clutched to his chest.

"Yes, we'd love to help."

"Wonderful!" said Perry. "Now, what we're initially looking for are first editions…"

"Quite right, Peregrine," said Mrs Glessing, entering from the hallway. "First editions."

Kate would have raised an eyebrow, but the sound of someone shouting on the terrace interrupted them.

They went out through the library's French doors onto the terrace where the lad from the stables was in a state of distress. At first, his cries were garbled, but they quickly became chillingly clear.

"There's been an accident. I think the lady's dead."

Imelda appeared from the sitting room onto the terrace. She had been crying. Kate struggled to take it all in, but there was really no time to think as they followed the distraught boy towards the stables.

Nine

Kate, Jane and Perry passed through the archway beneath the clock tower to enter a large, cobbled, rectangular courtyard with stables on all sides. Across the yard were stationed two unattended carts. One had timber and tools on board. The other carried a metal water tank.

Kate was more familiar with the simple type of stabling – a line of half doors, often with the top half open and a friendly horse peering out. Five Oaks was a much grander affair, with each side having three sets of large double doors with half-moon glazed fanlights above them facing onto the courtyard. This enabled the horses to be housed in stalls inside the building away from cold drafts.

The double doors farthest on the right were open.

"I'm not going in there again," said the boy.

Both Kate and Jane looked back to the archway to see who else might be coming. As it was, the next arrival was a thin, wiry chap in his fifties with a bushy moustache, brown trousers and an almost matching waistcoat. He had an unlit pipe in his right hand and a bemused look on his face. There was no time for questions though because Archie Hammond arrived followed by David Marston and Major Tipton.

"Webster? What's going on?" demanded Tipton.

The man with the pipe shrugged.

"I've no idea, Major. I've just come from my cottage."

Now that Webster was closer, Kate detected a faint whiff of alcohol. That was none of her business, of course.

"We should go in," she said.

"I'll hold the fort," said Perry.

Kate, Jane, and Tipton entered through the open doorway to stand in a straw-strewn gangway that ran both left and right. Facing them, from one end to the other, were stalls with horses occupying four of the eight, including the nearest, outside which a body lay on the ground.

Kate's heart began to thump hard. It was Eliza Cole, on her back, her eyes staring upward but seeing nothing.

"Right, get back," commanded the major. "This is no place for sightseers."

Kate and Jane followed him outside again where he pointed at Perry.

"Get to a telephone as fast as you can and call the police. Tell them Miss Cole has suffered a fatal accident. And somebody find Dr Evans!"

As it was, Dr Evans came hurrying into the courtyard.

"I'm here!"

Major Tipton instantly ushered him to the scene.

Kate felt helpless and was glad of her niece at her side.

"It's unthinkable, Jane."

"I know, Aunt, I know."

Dr Evans didn't take long to assess matters. He was with the stricken form for no more than a minute before returning to the doorway, from where he faced the small crowd.

"It was an accident then, Doctor?" prompted Tipton.

Dr Evans took a moment before answering.

"Yes, Miss Cole has met with a tragic, fatal accident," he announced. "Did anyone see what happened?"

None came forward.

"Very well," said the doctor. "My understanding is that Miss Cole was knocked by a horse causing her head to strike a post. Now if I could ask you all to leave. There's nothing to be done."

Major Tipton approached Jane and Kate with his arms out, as if shooing sheep away.

"A nasty accident. No reason to stay, ladies."

Kate wasn't at all keen on being herded away.

Just then, Jonathan Deerhurst and Lady Alsop entered the courtyard, the latter continuing through the stable doors, despite protests by both the doctor and the major.

She reappeared almost instantly.

"What on earth was Eliza doing in there?"

The doctor attempted to placate her.

"It was a tragic accident, Imelda."

"But Eliza rides Ariadne."

"Ah… yes."

"Ariadne's stabled over there," said Webster, indicating the opposite side of the courtyard.

"Eliza must have heard the other horse making a fuss," said the doctor. "No doubt she tried to help."

To Kate, he said it in a way that closed the matter too quickly. She also noticed how especially upset Mr Deerhurst seemed.

"Perhaps we should leave," she said, taking Jane's arm.

"Eliza knew all about horses," said Jane.

Kate sighed. "It's very upsetting, I know, but accidents do happen."

"It just seems a little off, that's all."

Aunt and niece paused beneath the archway from where Kate stared at the house – or at least its windowless flank facing the stables. Could they question the doctor? He didn't seem the type to welcome amateurs debating his methods, which Kate supposed was fair enough.

As it was, the doctor came by, heading back to the house.

"Dr Evans…?" asked Kate.

He stopped, although his manner suggested he wouldn't be stopping long.

"An utter tragedy," he said. "We can only pray for her soul. Now, if you'll excuse me, I must arrange for transportation to the morgue."

Any chance for Kate to pursue it further was lost as he strode off to the house.

Ten

Thirty minutes later, most guests were on the sunny terrace coming to terms with varying degrees of shock, while the equally dazed Brooke, Richards and Connie served tea and brandy in the dining room to those in need, which included themselves.

Perry Nash was with Kate and Jane.

"It's strange," he mused. "My work relates to those who have gone before us. It's just that…"

"A life cut short in the here and now?" suggested Kate.

He nodded. "We had that rotten business at Penford Priory and more of it around Lord Longbottom's passing, but it doesn't make it any easier."

"No… it doesn't."

His hand reached hers and squeezed.

Just then, two uniformed police officers appeared on bicycles at the side of the house nearest the stables. They laid down their bikes and approached the gathering. The elder of them introduced himself as Sergeant Nixon and his colleague as Constable Roberts. The sergeant had oiled grey hair and the long-suffering air of someone who had seen it all before. The constable was tall and looked inexperienced.

Major Tipton introduced himself and explained that he'd taken charge during the aftermath in the absence of any obvious authority. He also pointed out that Lady Alsop was resting and didn't wish to be disturbed.

"I see…" sighed the sergeant.

"I'll show you to the stables."

"All in good time, Major. Now, who found the unfortunate woman?"

"The stable lad. He's in the kitchen with a cup of tea, I think."

"And is the doctor still here?"

"He's resting in the morning room."

"Could somebody fetch them both?"

Brooke set off immediately. Meanwhile, Major Tipton turned to David Marston.

"Could you get Webster. I think he ought to speak."

Marston nodded and set off for the stables.

In short order, Dr Evans, Webster and Billy were on the terrace ready to face the sergeant's questions.

"What's your name, lad?"

"Billy Moresby."

"You found the body, did you?"

"Yes."

"Did you touch anything or move anything?"

"No! I saw her and I ran for help. That's it."

"Did you see anything of it?"

"No, I was filling the water tank from the stream. I thought I wasn't needed."

"That's fine. Did you see anyone go near the stables?"

"No, you can't see the stables from the stream. I only saw Mr Stamford. He was by the stream too. He said he was wondering what the fishing was like, but I could tell he was only there to enjoy a smoke away from his boss."

"Mr Stamford is my valet," explained the major.

"I see." Nixon turned to Webster. "And you're Mr Webster, are you?"

"Brian Webster, yes. I'm in charge of the stables."

"I trust nothing's been moved?"

"No, nothing at all – apart from the body."

The sergeant's eyebrows shot up.

"What?"

"I placed the body on the cart, covered it, and pulled it round to the front of the house ready for the morgue. You must have passed it."

"Who the blazes gave you permission to move the deceased?"

"She was disturbing the horses."

"You shouldn't have moved her."

"Why not? Dr Evans said it was an accident."

Nixon huffed with irritation.

"So, Doctor, what do you think happened?"

"It's quite straightforward. Eliza Cole went into an agitated horse's stall, the horse got spooked and jumped at her, knocking the poor girl's head against a post."

"The horse is Max, a four-year-old stallion," said Webster. "He can be a handful sometimes."

"I've called the mortuary," added the doctor. "A van is on its way. It was an accident. The coroner will concur."

Jane stepped forward.

"Excuse me, Sergeant, I'm Jane Scott. I knew the deceased. You ought to know something isn't right."

"Miss Scott. You heard the doctor. It was an accident."

Kate stepped in.

"Lady Jane is here representing her father, the Earl of Oxley, and she has some concerns."

Neither Kate nor Jane enjoyed pulling social rank, but on occasions it came in handy.

Sergeant Nixon sighed.

"*Lady* Jane… what seems to be the problem?"

"Eliza was a knowledgeable horsewoman. It's unlikely she'd go into the stall of a restless stallion."

Nixon looked her up and down as if inspecting a rotten gatepost.

"Are you a medical expert?"

"No."

"Then kindly refrain from interfering."

Nixon turned to the constable.

"Roberts, you stay here and keep order. I want to take a look at the scene. Billy, you come with me. I want you to show me what you saw when you got there."

Constable Roberts swung into action, urging Kate and Jane to go and get a cup of tea.

"Is that it?" said Jane.

Kate shared her niece's frustration.

"It would appear so," said Perry.

Kate looked out across the Five Oaks estate to the open countryside beyond. It was a sunny afternoon, spring was underway, and the rural landscape was waking up. It was a scene of renewal.

And yet…

A young life had been cut short. It was most probably a mishap, but something tugged at Kate's thoughts. Lady Alsop had a problem, one that Mrs Glessing felt the police should take a look at. And now there was a death. Could it just be a horrible coincidence?

She pulled Perry and her niece away from the crowd.

"What do you really think, Jane?"

"I think there's more to this than meets the eye. Eliza was going to share some news and there was the matter that may have warranted a call to the police."

"You really believe something doesn't add up," said Perry.

"In a way, I'm saying something *might* add up, but we're not seeing it."

"Worth looking into then?" said Kate.

"Definitely, Aunt."

"Should we mention Imelda's private matter to Sergeant Nixon? Or hold off until we know more?"

"The latter," said Jane. "Let's see if we can find out a bit more before we decide on the best course of action."

Eleven

The sitting room at Alsop House boasted a stone fireplace and two sizeable, if somewhat tired, red leather sofas separated by a Persian-style rug. The walls were adorned with a couple of tasteful countryside scenes in oil, while a crystal chandelier hung down from a high ceiling. Perhaps the main attraction should have been a polished silver trophy in a glass case – the Alsop Challenge Cup. But Kate and the professor paid it no heed.

An hour after the tragedy, they were having tea while waiting for Jane to join them. Jane herself had Imelda's permission to use the telephone in Sir Edgar's study opposite the library to call her chap, Harry Gibson.

"All rotten things aside, Perry, you must enjoy any opportunity to be in a library."

Perry smiled. "True… not that I'm getting much help from Antonia. I explained my passion for mediaeval history, and she passed me a copy of *Dracula*, which she assured me has an old castle in it."

Kate smiled sympathetically but wondered about the extent of his passion for history. Did it genuinely leave room for a having a woman in his life?

"I did come across something," said Perry. "A Victorian author of numerous volumes on minor Tudor figures. I don't think he's done much of a job though."

"A Victorian charlatan and his inferior volumes... oh dear."

"Oh, ignore me, Kate. It's not true. The fact is he's a perfectly good author and I'm jealous of him."

"Ah, you mean you'd love to tackle something like that yourself."

"Absolutely. He's written at least ten volumes. It's the sort of thing I'd love to do. I just never seem to find the time."

Kate had a brief vision of Perry in a study in Sandham-on-Sea happily typing up his latest work. But of course, Perry was tied to Oxford – a fact that reminded her of a mission to find the right moment to ask how serious he was about them being together.

Before she could utter a word though, Jane came in from the hallway.

"How did Harry take it?" asked Perry.

"He's worried."

"I'm not surprised."

"He offered to come down, but I told him I'm fine."

Kate wished Harry *would* come down.

"He's a good chap," said Perry. "One of the best. I know he'll be thinking of you the whole time until you're back with him."

Jane smiled. "I know."

"And *are* you fine?" asked Kate.

"More or less, Aunt. Same as you. What's really concerning me is the question of why Eliza entered that stall. It still feels wrong somehow."

"Well," said Kate, "if we're considering foul play, Jasper and Eliza's relationship might have come to a sudden end."

"Possibly," said Jane. "Jealousy, rage… I wonder if he has an alibi."

"Officially, he doesn't need one," said Perry. "It was an accident."

"*Officially*, yes," said Jane, "but let's not forget – the man declaring it an accident is Jasper's father."

"Yes, good point, Jane."

"We can't overlook it," said Kate. "A parent will go to any lengths to protect their child."

"What about footwear?" said Perry.

Kate and Jane stared at him.

"Well, footwear might whiff after a visit to the stables."

"True," said Jane, "although I'd suggest the stables are never cleaner than during the competition weekend. Unless you actually tread in something, then a walk across the grass would be sufficient. Besides, pretty much everyone entered the courtyard following the accident."

"Fair enough…"

"All is not lost," said Kate. "How about we consider everyone who had a connection to Eliza?"

"There are a few," said Jane. "Mind you, if we're looking at foul play, even if the competition goes ahead, any suspects will leave late tomorrow afternoon."

"We should also ask Imelda about Mrs Glessing's suggestion that she call in the police," said Kate. "There might be something there."

Jane sat down on a stool by the fireplace.

"We certainly don't have enough to trouble our friend at Scotland Yard."

Just then, David Marston breezed in.

"Sorry, I couldn't help but overhear. Eliza's death was a tragic accident. I really wouldn't get involved if I were you."

"Yes, of course," said Kate, having no desire to argue with him.

"What if the coroner disagrees with the doctor's opinion?" asked Perry.

"No chance," said Marston. "Dr Evans and the coroner are old friends. Unless you're suggesting incompetence on the doctor's part?"

"Nobody's questioning his ability," said Jane.

"What then?"

The conversation came to an abrupt halt at the sight of Dr Evans entering the room accompanied by Mrs Glessing.

"Dr Evans," said Kate by way of a welcome. "We're still in shock from what happened."

"Of course, Mrs Forbes. It's perfectly normal to feel a degree of shock after such an event. I can give you something for that, if you wish."

Kate had no intention of taking some hideous, overpowering sedative.

"No, I'm fine, thank you."

"It would give you twelve hours sleep in which to recover."

Mrs Glessing nodded her approval.

"Take a couple, Mrs Forbes."

Perry harrumphed.

"Kate has already taken a miracle cure. A cup of Earl Grey!"

Kate smiled. "It never fails."

"Such a strange accident," said Jane.

"Oh?" said Dr Evans. "How so?"

"Eliza had no reason to go into the wrong stable block. That horse wasn't likely to trust her. Even if it were playing up, she would have called for Webster or someone at the house."

The doctor seemed irritated.

"Perhaps the horse became tangled awkwardly."

"It wasn't tangled when we attended the scene."

"Why all the questions, Lady Jane? It was a tragic accident."

Kate wondered about the doctor's argument with his son, but Imelda entered the room with Archie Hammond. It appeared he was comforting her.

"Such a tragedy," said Hammond. "Imelda, take a seat. Rest yourself."

Kate decided it was time to act.

"I didn't know poor Eliza myself." She aimed her best questioning gaze at Antonia Glessing. "Who *did* know her?"

"Oh, um… let me see," said Mrs Glessing. "Imelda and myself. Lady Jane, of course. Major Tipton, Dr Evans, Jasper Evans, David Marston… and, to an extent, the staff."

Major Tipton entered.

"Ah, there you are, Imelda. Are you comfortable there?"

"I'm fine, Peter. Archie is looking after me."

Archie smiled.

Major Tipton did not.

"Has anyone seen my son?" said Dr Evans.

No one had.

Kate wondered about that. Where had he got to? She addressed Perry and Jane in a somewhat pointed manner.

"I think some rest in my room…"

With that, she left the sitting room followed by her niece and the professor.

In the hall, Kate was about to canvas for opinions on where they might find Jasper, but a voice engaged in a one-sided conversation captured their attention. Just out of sight, Miss Sophie Pearce was undoubtedly on the telephone in the vestibule.

The three of them froze and listened in.

"…I know… absolutely… I'll keep it to myself for now then… yes, I've already told them about the change of plan…"

Perry sneezed, which seemed to influence Miss Pearce's next utterance.

"I have to go," she said abruptly.

They heard the receiver being replaced followed by Miss Pearce heading up the stairs.

"Jasper Evans then," said Jane.

Kate spotted the maid.

"Connie? Sorry to trouble you. I don't suppose you've seen Jasper Evans?"

"He's in the grounds, Madam. I saw him from the kitchen window heading for the stream."

"That's very helpful. Thank you."

Connie smiled before entering a room farther up.

Perry thrust his hands into his pockets.

"If it's all right, I'll leave Jasper Evans to you. I'd like to finish what I started in the library. Otherwise, I'll never get away."

"Righto," said Kate. "We'll let you know if we learn anything."

Twelve

There were two gateways into the Five Oaks estate: the main one Kate and Jane used on their arrival, and a second one marked Deliveries & Trade. This second gate opened onto a track that ran along by the woods and gave vehicles access to the stables and the estate cottages.

Enjoying the time before sunset, at the end of the track, Kate and Jane came across these small, thatched cottages with whitewashed walls.

"I wonder which one's Mr Webster's place," said Kate.

Jane studied the small buildings, as if something about their appearance intrigued her.

"Interesting," she finally uttered.

Kate said nothing. She thought they looked quite normal for estate cottages.

A woman appeared at the door of the nearest dwelling. She bore a quizzical look upon her weather-worn face.

"Mrs Webster?" guessed Kate.

"Yes?"

"Have you heard the news? A dreadful business at the stables…"

"Yes, my Brian told me."

"He's with you, is he?"

"No, he's gone out again."

"I don't suppose you saw or heard anything unusual an hour or so ago?"

"No, I was coming back from Hillside Farm. I was getting wool, see. I'd been meaning to get over there as I'd been running low."

"You've not long returned then."

"Half an hour. As you say, a terrible business."

"Are the other cottages occupied?"

"No, two are empty. The other one's for Mr Russell, the groundsman, but him and his wife are away."

"Yes, I heard something about his sister, Rosie, having trouble with her knee."

"That's right. There's not much escapes you, is there."

"Oh, I'm sure there is," said Kate before bidding her farewell.

A short while later, aunt and niece stopped by the woods and enjoyed a moment in the countryside. The air, the birdsong…

"Sounds like a chiffchaff, Jane."

"It is. I can't see him though…"

Kate delved into her handbag for a small paper bag.

"Fancy a mint?"

"Ooh, just the thing, thanks."

They sucked their sweets and walked on towards the stream. For Kate, such moments were precious.

Farther up, a low fence ran along the far side of the modest watercourse – a boundary marker more than any attempt to keep anyone out. Jasper Evans was sitting on it smoking a cigarette. His shoes were wet from the shallow crossing.

"Lovely light at this time of day," he observed as they approached.

"You might remember me," said Jane. "We played here some years back."

"You'll be Lady Jane Scott," he declared.

"That's right."

"It was an easy guess. Everyone knew you'd be here. Mrs Glessing couldn't stop jabbering on about it."

"You haven't changed," said Jane.

Jasper laughed.

But his laughter died away.

"You have. Wouldn't have recognized you."

"This is my aunt, Mrs Kate Forbes."

"Hello, Mrs Forbes. I'd ask if you were enjoying your stay, but that's not likely in the light of events."

"You've heard then," said Jane. "Only, you weren't around when Eliza was discovered."

"I saw Webster. Then I went to see my father."

Kate wondered. Was he up to his neck in this? He did seem sad though.

"I can't believe what's happened," he added.

"None of us can." Kate stared into the water. She supposed the quiet stream found its voice during rainy periods. "Did you see Eliza heading to the stables?"

Jasper threw his half-smoked cigarette to the ground and jumped down off the fence to step on it.

"No, I didn't see anything. Why are you asking?"

"We're trying to build a picture," said Jane.

"A picture of what? It was a freakish rotten accident."

"You had a heated argument with your father," prompted Jane.

"So?"

"Was it about Eliza?"

Jasper said nothing, so Jane pushed on.

"Is it fair to say she ditched you? That's what we've heard."

"I don't care much for what you've heard, Jane. Eliza's death was an accident."

"What if it wasn't?"

Jasper puffed out his cheeks.

"On that basis, you'd have David Marston arrested."

"Would we?" said Kate.

"He had a thing for Eliza. I mean I'm going back a couple of years, but she rejected him."

"I see," said Jane. "Eliza finished with you, so David might have seen a second chance."

"And suffered a second rejection, yes. There's only so much certain men can stand. But, as I pointed out, it was an accident."

"We're not convinced it was," said Kate. "We're wondering if…"

But Jasper cut her off.

"I've no idea what Eliza was doing in Max's stall, but it sounds like you're challenging my father's competence, which I won't have."

"We're not challenging anyone's competence," Kate assured him. "It's more that he might have overlooked something, that's all."

Jasper glowered at them.

"What exactly are you suggesting?"

"We're not suggesting anything. We only want to make sure the truth of what happened is known."

"The truth? You mean you suspect Eliza's death wasn't an accident and that I might have something to do with it."

Jane cut in.

"You and your father argued earlier. You still haven't said what it was about."

"It had nothing to do with Eliza. It was a family matter, and it was quickly settled. Frankly, I find your questions irritating. Eliza was a dear friend, and my father is a highly regarded professional. I suggest you leave any speculation to the proper authorities."

69

Jasper stormed off, leaving Kate to reflect.

"It doesn't take a Scotland Yard detective to work out that we've annoyed him."

"That mustn't stop us, Aunt."

"No, it mustn't. Perhaps a little more tact though."

Kate and Jane set off back towards the house.

"How about going back to the scene, Jane? If it's quiet, we might learn something."

"Good idea, Aunt."

Thirteen

Kate and Jane paused in the arched entrance to the stables beneath the clock tower. From there the outward view was of the side of the house. On their earlier visit, the shock of Eliza's death made the view meaningless. Now, Kate took in the brick gable end wall dominated by two fat chimney stacks rising in parallel from the ground. Nearer the top of the building, these stacks turned diagonally to meet and merge into a single gable-end chimney stack topped with four large pots.

For Kate, the main feature was the absence of any windows.

In the courtyard, both carts had gone – one moved by Webster to the front of the house, the other most likely stored away behind one of the facing sets of doors. The tools and timber from the work cart were on the ground.

Now that Kate had time to take it all in, the place seemed run down. Certainly, the doors needed repairs.

"Shall we?" said Jane.

They entered through the doorway farthest on the right.

With time to study the environment, Kate noted how the fanlight windows over the double doors not only let in light but were opened inward a good few inches to let in fresh air. On the opposite wall, against which the stalls were aligned, there were high letterbox windows that were also open. Clearly, circulation was important.

"They've moved Max," said Jane, spotting the stallion in a stall farther down to the right.

Again, with time to look closer, Kate noted that Max's vacated stall was larger than most of the others. Special treatment for a prize stallion? No doubt Max's new stall was also a spacious one.

Jane, meanwhile, had crouched in front of the empty stall where Eliza had fallen.

"A patch of water, Aunt."

"Jane, there was a live animal there."

Jane bent closer and sniffed, which was beyond what Kate would have done.

"There's no scent. It's definitely water. Except there was no water here when we first looked."

Kate, now curious, crouched down too. While the space in front of the stall was largely straw-free, plenty of the stuff had been pushed up against the sides.

"Hello…"

She reached for the tip of something that didn't belong. Brushing it free of damp straw, she showed it to Jane.

"A cufflink, Aunt? What's that doing here?"

"We could ask Mr Webster."

Jane thought for a moment.

"Let's not. At least not until we're a little clearer on what happened."

"It won't be much use for fingerprints."

"No, but hang on to it."

Jane got up and peered into the next stall along. And the next.

"There's a bucket here… half full of water."

Kate turned to a back door.

"Another way out, Jane?"

"Yes… I do recall it from earlier visits."

Jane tried the final stall before the back door. A moment later, she held up a rusty iron bar.

"What do you make of this?"

Kate had never handled one before, but knew of its many names: crowbar, pry bar, jemmy…

"It's wet, Jane. I mean the rust is damp."

"And yet the straw here is dry. A likely implement for murder? Perhaps washed clean after the act?"

"Could it be that simple? An iron bar and a cufflink?"

"Well, I doubt we'll get to perform Cinderella with the cufflink, Aunt."

Kate concurred. "If a killer lost it, they'd no doubt get rid of the other one. And it's quite plain. Modern, perhaps.

Well, not old-fashioned, anyway. I'll stick my neck out and say the cufflink isn't going to solve the matter for us."

"Probably not, but if we keep quiet, it might yet give us an advantage."

Jane tried the back door, which was straightforward as it had already been unbolted. A light shove had it swing open onto a space at the back of the stable block.

Kate peered out. There was a mound of manure off to one side.

"That's good fertilizer, Aunt. I'd imagine they use in in the fields."

"Yes, that would make sense."

Ahead, a rough track went past a large exercise paddock to join a bigger track – the one for deliveries and trade that ran one way to the lesser gate and the other to the estate cottages.

They came back inside and pulled the door shut.

"A crowbar then, Aunt."

"Wouldn't a killer take it outside and throw it away?"

"Possibly, but would you want to be seen with it? It's not as if it's easy to hide it under clothing without leaving incriminating marks."

They returned to the courtyard.

"I wonder who was using the work cart earlier?" said Kate.

"It looks like fence repairs," said Jane, perusing the materials that were previously on it.

"Perhaps Mr Webster is responsible for the competition fences," said Kate. "Just as well he was at home at the time of Eliza's death. Otherwise, we might suspect him."

Just then, they noticed a boy watching them from the courtyard entrance.

.

Fourteen

"Hello," said Kate with a smile. "It's Billy, isn't it?"

He still looked shaken, which caused Kate to let out a sympathetic sigh. Sometimes bad things happened and all you could do was try to reassure those affected and bring those responsible to justice.

"Billy, I'm Kate and this is Jane. It was a rotten thing to happen here, wasn't it. I know you're still upset."

The boy gave a slight nod.

"I know you didn't see what happened. You told us you were at the stream."

"Yes, I was."

"You said you were getting water."

"Yes."

"You took a horse and cart, didn't you."

"No."

"No?"

"I pull the cart. It's not heavy."

"I see… well, before you went to the stream, did you see anything unusual"

Billy shook his head. It was obvious he was scared.

"Billy… we know Miss Cole was a good horsewoman. I'm certain she wouldn't have gone in there with a strange horse."

"No," said Billy. "She wouldn't. Max gets restless."

"I see he's been moved."

"Mr Webster moved him. He didn't touch anything though. He weren't sure if he should. The police and all… I haven't cleaned up yet. Do you think I should?"

"Perhaps ask Mr Webster to ask Major Tipton first."

"Right…"

Kate wondered how they might learn more.

"Well, these are sizeable stables, Billy. What can you tell us about them."

"Oh… well… there's stabling on the two sides. That's stalls for sixteen horses all told, and two bigger boxes for sick horses and expectant mares." He then indicated the stables opposite the scene of the fatal incident. "There's a hayloft above the stalls up there. It's made up for four stable hands to sleep in but there's only me."

"What about this side?" asked Kate, indicating the side of the yard opposite the entrance.

"That's harness rooms, a washroom, and carriage and cart housing."

"I have to say, Five Oaks stables is quite a set-up."

"We grow our own feed too. Five fields we got. Rye, wheat, barley, oats…"

He seemed a little more at ease now.

"I've heard horses eat lots of oats."

"Only if they're hunters or racehorses. It's the right amount of grain matched to the work they do. That's the thing. Like, a plough horse has barley, 'cos it keeps them going longer. You need to learn the right mix. Have you heard of forage? It's not all grass and hay. They need peas, beans, all sorts. Oh, let me tell you what they love. When carrots, beets and swedes are in season, yes please! And fresh grass too, 'cos they don't go out to pasture…"

"I can see you enjoy working here," said Kate.

"Yes, I do. My mum says I should be grateful. I'm up at four in the morning for grooming, feeding and mucking out, but plenty have it harder. I'm not sure now though. I mean I love to exercise them in the paddock, but… well… things have changed since her ladyship sold Pippa. The mood's gone sour and no mistake."

"Who's Pippa?"

"Lady Alsop's horse. The one she rides."

Kate was surprised. A glance at Jane told her she wasn't alone.

"Lady Alsop sold her horse?"

"A few months back."

Kate had been under the impression that Lady Alsop had lost her pet horse – lost meaning a fatality.

"Hello! Can I help?"

They turned to see Brian Webster arriving. He was carrying his jacket over his shoulder and had his shirt sleeves rolled up.

Kate smiled.

"Ah, Mr Webster."

"Off with you, Billy-Boy," he ordered – at which the boy hurried away and out of the courtyard.

With little daylight left, Kate didn't want to delay matters. Therefore, she chose not to mention meeting Mrs Webster.

"You weren't here at the time of the accident?" she asked plainly.

"No," he answered equally plainly.

Jane showed him the iron bar.

"We found this in the stall nearest the back door."

Webster took it and felt its weight.

"My crowbar. Handy for fence work."

He threw it onto the pile of odds and ends that had been removed from the cart.

Kate was a little annoyed. That item was evidence in… an accidental death.

"You were at your cottage?" asked Jane.

"Yes, I was. You'll be Lady Jane Scott, I believe, and Mrs Forbes, the aunt."

"Yes, that's right."

"Word gets around."

"I'm assuming you've met my father," said Jane.

"Yes, many times."

"I'm here in his place."

"Yes, I was informed about it yesterday."

"Have you worked here long?" asked Kate.

"Thirty years, man and boy, aside from a time in the army during the War. That was looking after horses too."

"You love horses then."

"I respect them, I understand them."

"I expect the competition weekend brings a few challenges for you."

"To a point, yes. It was once a much grander business, mind."

"More competitors, you mean?"

"When I started at Five Oaks, it was twenty horses challenging for the Cup. We only had stabling for sixteen, so some were placed in a temporary shelter."

"But that's all changed."

"Sir Edgar liked to keep up the tradition, but what started with twenty ended up with ten under him, and now it's down to eight."

"Is there the will to keep it going?"

"That's not for me to say."

Kate could see that the stables weren't exactly in tip-top condition. Were they actually heading for closure?

"The stables once held sixteen horses then," she said.

"During the competition weekend, yes. Local competitors would bring their own horses. Some still do.

We're expecting a few in the morning, though I'm not too sure if that'll happen now."

"A great pity."

"Yes, we were meant to have villagers coming up to enjoy the afternoon. We serve free tea and cake from the cart. I'll have to wash it down, of course. Been in use putting up the competition fences and... well... the other business."

"What horses are here now?" asked Kate, not wishing to dwell on the cart's current use.

"On this side, Lady's Alsop's stallion, Max, where the accident happened. Nero – that's Mr Deerhurst's horse. Apollo – that's the major's. Then Horatio. That's one of Lady Alsop's."

"The one David Marston is due to ride."

"Yes."

"Are they all stallions?" asked Jane.

"No, only Max. The others are geldings."

"And what about the other stable block? Mares, I presume."

"Yes, both of 'em Lady Alsop's. Jasper Evans' ride, Misty, and Ariadne."

"The horse Eliza Cole preferred."

"Yes."

"Not many Alsop horses then."

"Just the four."

To Kate, it seemed an irreversible decline for the stables.

"That must worry you."

Webster looked around, perhaps sadly.

"Before the War, horses would be ready for all-comers: riders, carriage journeys, staff delivering messages but... let's just say the spirit of the old place has changed. Once, we had a head groom, a stable hand and three stable boys. Now it's just me and Billy. The footman at the house lends a hand if need be."

"Very little stays the same over time," said Kate.

"No, indeed."

"How well did you know Eliza Cole?" asked Jane.

Webster considered it.

"She's been to Five Oaks a dozen times or so. I don't mix with Lady Alsop's guests though."

"You didn't speak with her today then?"

"Why are you asking?"

"Eliza and I were at school together," stated Jane.

"Oh... I'm sorry to hear it. I can't help you though. As I said before – I was at home. I came back here and saw what you saw."

"Mr Webster, think carefully. Did anything strike you as suspicious?"

"No, of course not. It's a tragedy, nothing more."

"We're just trying to work out why Eliza went to Max's stall, that's all."

"I expect he was unsettled. It seems to me Miss Cole tried to placate him."

Jane shook her head.

"Max is prone to restlessness. It's not out of the ordinary. Eliza would have known that."

"I don't know what you want me to say. It was a terrible accident. Why can't you accept it like I do?"

Jane gave up and so did Kate. They thanked Brian Webster and left the courtyard.

Outside, Kate voiced her concerns.

"Would you say those stables have a future, Jane?"

"I doubt they'll still be open by the end of the summer. I can't see how that links to Eliza's death though."

"Can we eliminate Mr Webster from any inquiry? He says he was at his cottage at the time."

"Mr Webster is hiding something."

"We have a cufflink. Do you think it's his?"

"I don't know. Something's not right though. If he *were* at his cottage, how do we explain his arrival at the stables from the wrong direction?"

"The wrong direction? Are you sure, Jane?"

"Yes, definitely."

Fifteen

Kate and Jane reached the terrace to find Perry Nash outside the library's French doors. The sun, sitting just above the horizon, appeared to set the red bricks of the house ablaze.

"Thought I'd enjoy the sunset," he explained. "Where have you been?"

"Exploring," said Kate.

"Find anything interesting?"

Kate lowered her voice.

"A potential murder weapon."

"Oh?"

Perry looked genuinely shocked.

"A rusty crowbar. We found it in the stables. The rust was damp as if someone had doused it in water with a purpose."

"To remove fingerprints?"

"Possibly, although Mr Webster's fingerprints wouldn't mean much. He works there."

Perry concurred.

"We'd need something more suspicious to consider him a killer."

"There might be something," said Jane. "He said he came from his cottage to the scene of the so-called accident – but he arrived from the wrong direction."

A thought occurred to Kate.

"He'd been drinking. I could smell it on his breath. Do you think he was coming back from the pub?"

"Is there a pub nearby?" asked Perry.

"We drove past one on the way here," said Jane. "The Royal Oak in Lower Fincham – a mile or so in the right direction if you were going to the stables from there."

Perry raised an eyebrow.

"It would be easy enough to check the pub… assuming the locals aren't suspicious of outsiders… which they most probably are… meaning it wouldn't be as easy as I just said."

"Aunt found a cufflink at the scene," said Jane. "An unremarkable one admittedly."

Kate showed it to Perry.

"Hmm… I doubt I can recall what anyone's cufflinks look like, especially when we're all wearing jackets. There's another factor, of course. If it were foul play, the killer would have lost the other one as soon as he could."

"Let's not narrow it down to a man," said Jane.

"Ah, you mean it might have been a woman wishing to throw any nosy investigators off the scent. Yes, I can see that."

"We're keeping it to ourselves for now," said Kate. "Just in case."

Perry nodded. "Good thinking. If it's murder, why let the killer know our hand."

"Precisely."

"That said, we shouldn't rule out the official explanation. An accident may yet prove to be the case."

"True," said Kate.

"An iron bar and cufflink though… where was Eliza's horse kept in relation to where she was found?"

"Ariadne is stabled on the opposite side of the courtyard."

"Nowhere near Max then."

"No, well, Max is a stallion."

"Ah… and Ariadne is… yes, sorry. My everyday knowledge of keeping horses is sparse at best, but I think I've grasped that stallions and mares are kept separate."

"Yes," said Jane. "Some of the horses are geldings, but they're no trouble."

Perry's brow furrowed.

"Geldings are… am I right in thinking they're male horses… except they've been… so they're unable to…?"

"Precisely," said Jane, "which results in a good temperament. You can place a gelding with other geldings, mares or stallions. You can't say the same for a feisty stallion."

"Yes… ahem…" Perry seemed ready to move on.

"How does the estate compare with your earlier visits?" asked Kate, helping him.

"Oh, well, I was only sixteen last time I was here, Kate. I doubt I paid much attention to how things were." He paused for a moment. "That said, there are fewer staff. I think that's noticeable. I'm sure there was a housekeeper and three or so maids. I suppose…"

He paused again.

"What is it, Perry?"

"Alsop House is *trying* to be the same as it's always been, but my memories go back to Sir Edgar's parents. To me, it was full of joy back then. Now it seems full of an effort to *create* joy… if that makes sense. Something's definitely been lost."

Perry snapped out of his reverie.

"Sorry, I'm not helping much. If we genuinely suspect foul play, we need to find a connection between Eliza and her killer. If we do, we might find a motive. Otherwise, we might have to accept it was an accident."

"A connection then," pondered Kate. "Perry, perhaps you could help us?"

"Yes, of course, Kate. In what way?"

She still enjoyed hearing him say her name.

"How well did everyone here know Eliza? If this was foul play, we don't have much time."

"Yes, I see. I'd imagine the competition will be cancelled and everyone will be off home."

"Learn what you can, perhaps starting with Imelda. We ought to ask her about Mrs Glessing's suggestion that she should call in the police. It might be nothing. Or it might have a bearing on what happened."

"Imelda then."

From within the library, Mrs Glessing appeared at the French doors with her broadest smile.

"Perry, *really*, if you need anything at all from Imelda, let me help you."

"Oh righto," said Perry, returning perhaps a less enthused grin.

"We'll rest in the sitting room," said Kate.

"Oh, I wouldn't if I were you, Mrs Forbes. Jasper's in there – in a foul mood."

"Ah right."

"He really is a complete failure, you know."

Kate was surprised at this woman's capacity to say anything at any time. Bolts from the blue, no less.

"Is he?" she queried.

"You might have seen one of his early paintings in here."

Kate peered beyond Mrs Glessing to the picture on the wall.

"Oh yes, very nice."

"Yes, very nice, as you say – and not at all like the rubbish he paints nowadays, which explains why he works behind the counter of an Eastbourne pharmacy on a low wage."

"Right…"

"This way, Professor."

As she lured Perry inside, the last thing Kate heard was Mrs Glessing being cheerful.

"Do you know, I haven't visited Oxford in absolutely ages…"

Jane nudged her aunt.

"You're not to worry about Mrs Glessing."

"Aren't I?"

"No."

"I won't then."

"Now… did you notice how upset Jonathan Deerhurst was when he learned what had happened?"

"You mean we should have a word with him?"

"Yes."

"Where might we find him?"

"Miss Pearce would know. I wonder if she's still working in the drawing room."

Sixteen

Rather than surprise Miss Sophie Pearce by appearing at the drawing room French doors, Kate and Jane went via the hallway. This took them past the sitting room, where a quick glance through the open door revealed Jasper in conversation with Archie Hammond.

They continued to the next room where they found Miss Pearce using a side table as a makeshift desk.

"We're not disturbing you, are we?" said Kate with a hopeful smile.

"No, no," said Sophie, rising from her seat. "I was just off to my room."

"We were hoping to speak with Mr Deerhurst. Before we do though, could we ask you a few questions? If you don't mind?"

Sophie's expression suggested this wouldn't be likely.

"Unfortunately, I have a headache."

"May I ask how long you've been Mr Deerhurst's personal secretary?"

"Not very long. A year or so."

"Ah…"

"I worked for his father for twelve years."

"Ah."

"By the by," said Jane, "did you resolve your problem of having to change your plans?"

"Pardon me?"

"We thought we heard you on the telephone?"

"No… not me."

With that, Miss Pearce left the room.

Kate and Jane exchanged a look and followed her.

They caught her climbing the stairs.

"Miss Pearce?" called Kate. "Before you retire, could you let Mr Deerhurst know we'd like to see him?"

She stopped on the half-landing and turned to face them below.

"He's resting in his room. He won't want to be disturbed."

"Were you alone at the time of the accident?"

Miss Pearce raised an eyebrow.

"Why would you ask that?"

"We're just trying to learn as much as we can about Eliza's death."

"May I ask why?"

Kate thought before answering.

"We're not suggesting Dr Evans has made a mistake, but we feel it's all been a little hasty. A deeper look might be worthwhile."

"Are you saying a crime has been committed?"

"I'm saying no-one has explained why Eliza was in Max's stall."

"I'm not sure I can help you. I know very little about horses."

Sophie Pearce seemed set to turn away, so Kate got in quickly.

"Did you know Eliza?"

This surprised Miss Pearce enough to stop her turning away.

"I met her for the first time today. I believe she was a civil service secretary."

"Is that so?" said Jane. "The sort of job that requires an ordered mind."

"I suppose so."

"She mentioned advising you on the latest fashions," said Kate.

"Did she?"

"Yes, she did," said Jane.

"Oh… yes… she made one or two suggestions. It's not something that interests me though."

"Ah," said Kate, unsure of what this told them.

"She seemed a nice young woman," added Miss Pearce.

"She was," said Jane. "I knew her a little from school."

"I'm sorry for your loss, Lady Jane. It's a tragedy."

Once again, Sophie Pearce looked set turn away and continue up the stairs.

"The competition," said Kate. "If it goes ahead, will Mr Deerhurst compete? No one was more upset than him."

Sophie sighed.

"I doubt Mr Deerhurst will take part."

"Miss Pearce is right."

All turned to Jonathan Deerhurst at the banister on the landing at top of the stairs.

"Sorry, my door was open. I heard voices. I won't compete after what's happened. I'll return to London."

Despite the growing crick in her neck, Kate seized the moment.

"Mr Deerhurst, did you not think it strange that Eliza was in the wrong part of the stables?"

"Oh…?"

"Eliza rode Ariadne who was in the other block."

"That's right, she did. But… what are you suggesting?"

"Eliza was a knowledgeable horsewoman."

"Accidents happen, Mrs Forbes."

"Yes, they do. But we're suspicious of this one. Something doesn't add up."

Miss Pearce cut in.

"Surely we shouldn't be questioning an experienced professional such as Dr Evans."

But Kate's gaze was fixed on Miss Pearce's employer.

"Mr Deerhurst? Did you know Eliza Cole well?"

"Why do you ask?"

"You were particularly upset earlier."

He hesitated before answering.

"I was."

"We heard you were checking some fences at the time Eliza was killed."

Sophie stepped in again.

"Mr Deerhurst doesn't have to explain himself to anyone."

"It's all right, Miss Pearce. Yes, I was over on the far side by the woods."

"Did anyone see you there?" asked Kate.

He thought for a moment.

"I don't think so. In fairness, I wasn't paying much attention to the rest of the grounds."

"Was there genuinely a problem with the competition fences?"

"Not the fences; the landing areas. The weather's been dry which can make the ground too firm. I was going to ask Mr Webster to move a couple for a softer landing."

"Thanks," said Jane. "We're just trying to find out if anyone saw anything unusual. Eliza deserves a proper effort. At least, that's what Aunt Kate and I think."

Deerhurst mulled it over.

"Perhaps there's something in what you say. It does seem to have been decided rather quickly."

"We may have found a weapon," said Kate. "An iron crowbar. Someone removed it from the cart in the yard. It was left by the back door of the stables."

"I see," said Deerhurst.

"Shouldn't it be left to the police?" asked Miss Pearce.

"Not necessarily," said Deerhurst. "The police won't act unless something specific forces them to do so. I'll delay my return to London. If I can help, I will."

Kate was pleased, although Jonathan Deerhurst had more to say.

"I'll also make some inquiries of my own. If it's murder, I think we already know the name of the killer."

Kate was stunned.

"Do we?"

"I'll say no more," said Deerhurst before turning away and heading along the gallery to the men's hallway.

Seventeen

If a killer lurked among them, there was no time to waste. With that in mind, Kate and Jane went to join Jasper Evans and Archie Hammond in the sitting room. Regardless of Jonathan Deerhurst's claim to know the killer, they had a responsibility to Justice that meant them identifying their own suspects.

On entering, they noticed Jasper outside on the terrace, lighting a cigarette and possibly sulking.

"A restful long weekend, Mr Hammond?" asked Kate as she and Jane settled on the sofa opposite Archie Hammond, who looked very comfortable with his jacket open and his feet crossed.

"Yes," he replied, "six or seven days here was just what I needed."

He caught Kate glance at the buttons on his shirt straining a little against his tummy. Indeed, he patted his middle.

"Cake, cake and more cake, Mrs Forbes. It's tough work."

Kate chuckled. "You have my sympathy. It's an ongoing battle for us all. Lady Alsop is a fine host."

"Yes, I do believe it's an Alsop tradition."

"You must have got on well with Sir Edgar," prompted Jane.

"Ah, Cousin Edgar, yes. He and Imelda were two peas in a pod. Most people never got to know them properly, but I did. I knew their little ways."

"You were close friends then."

"Yes, we were... although, to be perfectly honest, I haven't been close enough to Imelda since Edgar passed away."

"Ah."

Hammond removed his glasses and began cleaning them on a handkerchief.

"Things change though," he said. "It's certainly a change being here again. For us who live in London, it's easy to forget the joys of a slower pace in the country."

"You're enjoying Five Oaks then," said Kate.

He put his glasses on again.

"I'm rather taken with it, Mrs Forbes. Who knows, perhaps it's the sort of life I could settle into."

"Is there a Mrs Hammond?" asked Jane.

"No, I'm a lifelong bachelor. Or so I thought. I'm beginning to think differently on many things, Lady Jane."

David Marston breezed in from the hallway.

"All this hanging around! Once Lady Alsop cancels the competition, I'm heading back to Eastbourne."

"Before dinner?" questioned Kate.

"Would Lady Alsop want us to stay on?"

Kate had no idea. "Of course she would. Even if she might outwardly seem reluctant."

"Well, I'll see what Dr Evans decides. Neither him, me, nor Jasper were staying overnight, so it was always the plan to get a ride back to Eastbourne after dinner."

"You won't come back tomorrow then?"

"I did intend to, obviously, but there'll be no reason to if the competition is off."

This was exactly what Kate wished to avoid – to have potential suspects leave the estate and not return.

"Are you still against the doctor?" added Marston. "That's the whisper going around."

"We're only interested in the truth," said Kate.

"That's what we all want," said Marston.

Hammond sighed.

"That poor young thing…"

"You were in the library at the time," said Jane.

Hammond eyed her.

"Waiting for the professor, yes."

"Waiting quite a while."

"Well… perhaps fifteen minutes. It was no problem. I wanted to help him with those dusty old books."

"You were reading some documents while you waited."

"Contracts, yes. Why do you ask?"

"No reason. You mentioned working in the City of London."

"Yes, that's right."

David Marston spotted Jasper outside on the terrace, finishing his cigarette.

"Jasper…" he mused. "You wouldn't believe he set out to be a doctor like his father. Did you know he gave up on college to pursue art, and then messed that up too?"

Kate watched Jasper drop the stub to the ground, crush it underfoot, and stride off.

"Is that why Eliza gave up on him?"

"Oh… well… I wouldn't know about that. He's unreliable, that's the thing. He doesn't have prospects like I do."

"Is that what you told Eliza? That you have prospects?"

"I'm not sure what you mean, Mrs Forbes."

"We heard that you once had hopes with Eliza."

"Really? I don't know who told you that. Eliza and I… we barely knew each other. She certainly wasn't my type, that's for sure. Not that what happened wasn't… you know."

He turned to Archie Hammond.

"Say, you don't fancy a game of billiards, do you? I could do with a distraction before I leave."

Hammond smiled.

"Why not. It's a fair while until dinner anyway. Ladies, if you'll excuse us…"

Kate waited for them to leave before sharing her thoughts.

"I'm not sure that got us anywhere, Jane."

"I wouldn't say that, Aunt. We learned something important about Mr Hammond."

"Did we?"

"Yes, we learned he's lying about being in the library for fifteen minutes."

"Did we?"

"Yes, definitely. I'm not sure if he's our killer, but he's lying for a reason. Lady Alsop was visibly upset on the terrace at that time. It might be related to that."

"Shouldn't we have confronted him about it?"

"As far as the police are concerned, there hasn't been a murder. I'm thinking it might be best if we continue to keep our powder dry until we know more. Archie Hammond could be up to anything. Then again, so could David Marston."

"Honestly, Jane. I'm not sure how we should proceed."

"Nor me, Aunt. Perhaps we should check on the professor. He might have learned something."

Eighteen

They found Perry alone in the library, which pleased Kate.

"Did you get a chance to speak with Imelda?" she asked.

"No, she was tired, which is understandable. Before I shook off Antonia though, she confirmed a few things. She said hospitality drove the popularity of the Alsop Challenge Cup in the early days. There were three days of four-course lunches, seven-course dinners, and plenty of riding. Now, with so few staff, it's two days of sandwiches for lunch, a three-course dinner for a fraction of the original number, and the understanding that some of those who live nearby in Eastbourne don't stay overnight."

"Times change."

"True – although I actually like sandwiches and light dinners."

Kate smiled. If only she didn't have the other matter to contend with – the question of how two people can be together when they live 120 miles apart. It was a figure she knew from calculating it on a map of England three months earlier.

Any thought of sharing their latest theories though was halted by the sight of Major Tipton on the terrace with Lady Alsop.

"Well, I never," said Perry. "Imelda appears to be fully rested."

While the French doors were closed, it only took a turn of the handle for Kate to open them just a crack to 'let in some fresh air'.

Major Tipton was speaking, "…not beyond me, Imelda. I know more than enough about investments to make the right choices. There's a chap in the City…"

For whatever reason, Imelda led the major off the terrace into the dusk, and effectively out of earshot.

Kate recalled Imelda speaking earlier: "My investments are my business…" She'd been with Eliza Cole at the time.

Kate shared what she knew with Jane and Perry.

"Why don't we find out," said Jane.

Before Kate could question it, Jane was outside on the terrace with Kate following.

"Oh, Imelda, I didn't see you there," said Jane with a believable degree of surprise. "And Major. What a pleasant evening."

"It is," Major Tipton agreed. "If a little chilly."

Jane led Kate closer to the duo.

"Perhaps you could help us, Imelda?"

"If I can, I will, Jane."

"You'll have heard that Aunt Kate and I have some concerns about Eliza's death."

"And you'll know, dear Jane, that I won't question Dr Evans. He's a man of great experience."

"Absolutely, but perhaps you could clarify something for us. Mrs Glessing is certain that you should have called in the police regarding a different matter."

Major Tipton harrumphed but said nothing.

"That's private," said Imelda. "It has nothing to do with poor Eliza's death."

Kate cut in. "Is it possible Eliza was looking into something?"

"Kate, please, it was an accident."

"She spoke with you about investments. It might not mean anything, but…"

"Kate, really, you're making a fuss over nothing. Can we please close the subject."

Major Tipton grunted.

"I think Imelda has said more than enough on the matter. No more questions now, ladies. I must insist on it."

"Of course," said Kate.

She and Jane returned to the library, where Kate closed the French doors behind them.

"Any luck?" asked Perry.

"If you mean 'are we getting anywhere', then no," said Kate. "At least, it doesn't feel like it."

"Have heart, Aunt Kate. We're getting there," said Jane. "Slowly but surely."

But Kate was wondering about Major Tipton. Was he the right man for Imelda? Could he be trusted?

She shared the thought with Jane and Perry, the latter of whom urged caution.

"We're talking about Major Peter Tipton, until recently of the 11th Hussars, a greatly respected cavalry regiment known to all as Prince Albert's Own."

"Speaking of the major," said Jane. "Where was he when Billy called for help?"

"No idea," said Kate.

"He arrived quickly," said Perry. "Then he dictated how things went from there."

"Yes, he controlled the situation. Whether that—"

A knock at the French doors interrupted them.

Major Tipton entered.

"Imelda's returned to her room."

"Right," said Kate. "We never meant to upset her."

"No, of course not. Eliza's death deserves a thorough investigation. It's Webster I'm annoyed with. If he'd taken his job seriously, the accident wouldn't have happened."

"We're concerned for Imelda," said Kate.

"As am I," said the major.

"She's vulnerable."

"Vulnerable? Please bear a few things in mind, Mrs Forbes. Sir Edgar and I were great friends, Imelda means a lot to me, and I'm a man of independent means living in Eastbourne, where I'm on the golf club committee."

"We weren't suggesting anything untoward."

Jane cut in. "Major, you were with the doctor when he attended the scene of the accident."

"Yes."

"Can you explain how water appeared on the floor where Eliza fell."

"Water?"

"It appeared after her death."

"Well now… the doctor asked for water and a rag to wash the wound for a better look. It's all perfectly innocent, I'm sure. Now, I'm off to my room. I'll see you at dinner."

With that, he headed off into the hallway.

Kate wasn't happy.

"Water and a rag to wash the wound for a better look? Or to clean away any rust from a murder weapon?"

Perry sighed.

"If this is foul play, shouldn't we be looking for a motive?"

"We are," said Jane. "Perhaps it's time we made a telephone call, Aunt."

"To you-know-who? It's half past six. He won't be at Scotland Yard."

They headed to Sir Edgar's study opposite the library for privacy, from where Kate called Chief Inspector Ridley at home.

"Hello, Chief Inspector. It's Kate Forbes calling from Sussex. I bet you weren't expecting to hear from me on a Friday evening."

"No, I wasn't, Mrs Forbes. To what do I owe the pleasure?"

"There might be grounds for a Scotland Yard investigation at Alsop House near Eastbourne. That's where Jane, Peregrine Nash and I are spending the weekend."

"Oh... I was looking forward to a quiet weekend after a very long week at the Yard. What's up?"

"A young woman died due to an accident. That's the opinion of the doctor who attended the scene. It's just that we're not convinced. We suspect foul play."

"I see."

"There's more, Chief Inspector – some hidden business that might be of interest to the police. And we found a cufflink at the scene. And a potential murder weapon. We can't quite get to the bottom of it all yet though."

"I'm not quite with you. Has anyone from the local police force been to the house?"

"Yes, Sergeant Nixon and Constable Roberts came up from Eastbourne."

"Right... and what did the sergeant make of the doctor's opinion on the cause of death?"

"He accepted it without question."

"I see," said Ridley. He then fell silent, which Kate took for him considering their appeal.

"Well?" she prompted.

"I'm sorry, if you're telling me a qualified medical practitioner has verified the cause of death as an accident, and that the local police have accepted it, then it's a matter for the coroner. You can attend the inquest as witnesses, of course…"

"You won't come down to Sussex then."

"No, but by all means keep an eye on things. If anything significant comes up, you know where to find me."

Nineteen

Lady Alsop's guests began to gather for pre-dinner drinks in the sitting room. Kate and Jane arrived in eveningwear to find a few already present: Dr Evans, Jonathan Deerhurst, and Miss Pearce.

Both Kate and Jane accepted a small sherry from Connie, while Brooke stood by ready to step in where needed.

Almost immediately, Dr Evans made an effort with Jane.

"Do forgive me, Lady Jane, but I haven't asked after your father. How is Robert?"

"He's well, thanks – he's on business in Scotland. Hence me standing in."

"Ah yes, that's very sporting of you. As you know, we've been coming here for the Challenge Cup weekend since before the War. Jasper was due to compete, but now…?"

He gave a little shrug.

"You're not staying overnight though?"

"Oh, we're quite nearby. I'll drive myself, Jasper and David Marston back to Eastbourne later."

"Yes, of course."

Just then, Perry entered looking dapper in a formal grey suit with a dark green tie.

"I was wondering about the competition," he said generally. "Do we think it will go ahead?"

"I doubt it," said Jonathan Deerhurst. "I expect Lady Alsop will make an announcement soon enough."

"The tradition of the thing must make it hard to decide," said Dr Evans.

Kate wondered about that. A postponement seemed the right thing though.

Major Peter Tipton, looking dashing in a suit, entered with an "Evening all!"

He followed this up with a compliment about their host, Lady Alsop, who he said was just coming along the hallway.

Once again, Kate wondered. Was he the right man for Imelda?

A moment later, Lady Alsop, Mrs Glessing and Archie Hammond came in.

"Riding coat tails, eh Hammond?" said Tipton amid the general greetings.

"A sherry for Lady Alsop and Mrs Glessing," he instructed Brooke. "And one for me, too."

"Very good, Major."

Hammond smiled at Kate while flexing his neck and tugging at his collar and tie.

"Is it me, or is it hot in here?"

Kate didn't think it was hot. She wished someone would throw more coal on the fire. She then wondered if Archie was sucking up to Imelda. Was he reassuring her that the house was warm enough to protect her from any worry that her cost-cutting might be seen as mean? If Major Tipton was genuinely interested in Imelda, did he now have a serious rival for her affections?

"Ladies and Gentlemen," announced Lady Alsop. "I decided a short while ago that the competition will not go ahead. Telephone calls have been made to alert those due to arrive tomorrow. I'm sure we'll reconvene at some future date in happier circumstances."

All offered their complete understanding.

"Many apologies to you, Jane," she continued, turning to her special guest. "You so willingly came to represent your father in awarding the trophy."

Jane smiled. "It's perfectly fine, Imelda. I was due to take a break from my research studies and I'm always happy to represent my father. I'll do so again at Alsop House, if needed."

Imelda smiled and turned to Kate.

"And you, Kate? We've got you here for no reason. I'm sure you understand."

"Absolutely. I think it's for the best."

From there, more drinks were served and smaller conversations broke out. Among these, Imelda and Antonia Glessing joined Kate and Jane.

"What are you up to in Sandham, Kate?" asked Imelda. . "Perry mentioned something about you working to get more visitors."

Kate gave a brief outline of her mission to attract more visitors, and to have those visitors want to return again and again. Hence her co-ordinating improvements in amenities and persuading locals with money and/or time to get involved.

Jane added, "I keep suggesting that Aunt Kate should target a seat on the local council. She's just what Sandham-on-Sea needs."

"Ah," said Mrs Glessing, "so we could be looking at the next Mayor!"

"One step at a time," said Kate. "I do feel it's a worthwhile cause though."

She glanced at Perry chatting with Dr Evans, Jonathan Deerhurst and Miss Pearce. Could it really work for two people if one was a professor at Oxford and the other the Mayor of Sandham?

She then noticed Archie Hammond and Major Tipton having a quiet word in the corner. How might that work out for Imelda?

"Lady Jane," said Mrs Glessing, "may I say that while we miss your father's presence, you're an admirable representative of the Scott family."

"Thanks," said Jane. "My father was sorry he couldn't attend this year, and my brother, Alexander, as you might know, is in the army."

"Ah yes. Hopefully, he's enjoying army life."

"I'm sure he is. He's currently an adjutant to the military attaché at our embassy in Paris."

"Lucky Alex!" said Imelda.

Kate felt that Alexander had earned it. As a younger man, he fought all through 1918 as a second lieutenant on the front line.

"We're lucky to have you, Lady Jane," added Mrs Glessing. "At your age, I was married with two young children, which left me exhausted and unable to attend social gatherings. Do you have any plans in that direction?"

Kate felt like telling Mrs Glessing to mind her own business, but Jane got in first.

"We'll see."

Imelda glanced at her old friend.

"Antonia, we must let the younger generation make their own plans."

"Imelda, dear, I'm merely pointing out that marriage is a wonderful institution. I, myself, am not against considering it again. I've been a widow for seven years, which I feel is the right sort of interval if one loses one's husband. Mrs Forbes, I understand you lost yours only a few months ago?"

Kate was crestfallen.

"Nearly two years," she managed to utter.

Jane stepped in.

"Uncle Henry loved you to the ends of the earth, Aunt Kate. He'd want you to be happy and not mope about for years on end dressed in black."

"Not even two full years?" queried Mrs Glessing. "It must seem like only yesterday."

Kate knew Mrs Glessing's game – and so it seemed did Jane, whose voice lifted a little.

"Queen Victoria died a million years ago – well, alright, twenty-eight years ago, but that era has passed."

"Are we speaking of love, ladies?" It was David Marston, who had arrived unseen. "Perhaps you could answer a question for me."

Kate sighed. *Do we have to?*

But Marston pressed on.

"With your greater experience and wisdom, do you believe in love at first sight?"

Kate was a little taken aback but she felt the need to protect the other ladies from the intrusion.

"Mr Marston… I believe that sometimes *something* might happen at first sight. Perhaps it's a power that comes from within. It tells us that we're not against the possibility of forming a connection, despite having only just set eyes on the person in question."

Marston laughed. "It's not as catchy as love at first sight."

"Perhaps not. Is it something you've experienced for yourself?"

"Yes, very much so."

He smiled at Jane, which sent a cold shiver down Kate's spine. Thoughts flashed through her mind. Hadn't Marston had a thing for Eliza that was unwelcome? Didn't she reject him before she hooked up with Jasper Evans? When Eliza ditched Jasper earlier today, did David Marston perceive a second chance with Eliza? And did she reject him a second time?

She smiled at him.

"Who's the lucky lady?"

He answered Kate without his gaze leaving Jane.

"I couldn't possibly say at the moment."

Kate's smile remained fixed. Marston was the last man on earth Jane would consider. That aside, she wondered about Jane's chap, Harry. He should have been here at a time like this to have a word with Marston or possibly kick him up the backside.

Just as Kate reminded herself that she was wholly against violence, the dinner gong sounded.

As the company filed into the hallway bound for the dining room, Imelda caught the doctor's attention.

"Will Jasper be joining us?"

"I've no idea, Imelda. I'm not actually sure of his whereabouts."

"Perhaps he popped out for some fresh air."

"Yes, that might be it."

Kate knew that the non-staying guests had used a spare room upstairs to change for dinner. Was Jasper hiding up there? She decided if she were to tread carefully, she might be able to push the doctor a little.

"Dr Evans, that argument you and Jasper had earlier? He's not still upset about that, I hope."

Dr Evans was clearly unhappy with her line of questioning.

"Could we drop the matter, Mrs Forbes."

"Of course," said Kate.

Seems I didn't tread carefully enough!

Twenty

The dining room at Alsop House had many fine features, not least of all a grand oak fireplace, a highly polished mahogany dining table and a couple of oil paintings of wildflowers in bloom.

The table was long enough to seat fourteen diners at a pinch. As it was, twelve places had been laid for dinner, with Lady Alsop at the head of the table. To her left sat Perry Nash, Antonia Glessing, David Marston and Jane. To Lady Alsop's right sat Archie Hammond, Dr Evans, Sophie Pearce, Jonathan Deerhurst and Kate. At the far end of the table, facing Lady Alsop, was Major Peter Tipton. This was of course eleven, the missing guest being Jasper Evans, whose seat between Mrs Glessing and David Marston remained empty.

Kate looked across the table at Jane and up the other end to Perry sitting alongside Mrs Glessing.

Who was responsible for the seating arrangements?

"No sign of Jasper then," observed Jonathan Deerhurst.

David Marston perked up. "Had he and Eliza been here, we'd have thirteen..." But he trailed off.

During the soup course, Kate noted · Marston's imitation of a hungry walrus. Another thing she noted was a lack of discourse. It seemed no one wanted to start a conversation. After all, one of their fellow guests had met a tragic end. What would they discuss?

Imelda smiled at Perry Nash.

"I hope the books aren't too dull... or too dusty?"

"No, Imelda, not at all. The library has some interesting volumes. In the simplest terms, I'm looking for the earliest books I can find. Among other factors, of course."

David Marston interrupted while wiping soup from his chin with a napkin.

"Thomas Caxton. He's your man, Professor. Did you know he printed the first books?"

Perry smiled.

"Yes, *William* Caxton did develop a printing press in the 1470s. It wasn't without problems though, and I don't mean technical matters. Language itself was the problem."

"Language?" said Marston. "He printed books in English. Surely that's well known."

Imelda coughed politely.

"Perhaps you could explain, Perry. As much as I adore young David's enthusiasm, I do from time to time crave an intelligent guide."

Perry smiled. "Well, put simply, Caxton had to translate works. But into which language?"

"English," repeated Marston. "I've already said so, Prof."

Kate pondered if it would be acceptable to flick a spoonful of soup into Marston's stupid face. She supposed not.

Meanwhile, Perry continued.

"After the Norman Conquest of 1066, Middle English became our language for the next four hundred years. Of course, during that time, most people didn't travel, so by Caxton's time, our language had regional variations with wholly different words for things, and different ways of stringing them together. Does that fit with your understanding, Mr Marston?"

"What? Oh, yes. More or less."

Perry continued. "Take Caxton's 'eggs' anecdote. In his preface to the 1490 edition of his translation of Virgil's *Aeneid*, he recounts a scene he witnessed on the Thames riverside in Kent, having landed there with others by boat. It demonstrates the problem of language evolving differently between the north and the south. A northern chap from the boat asked a local southern woman if he might buy some eggs. The woman told him she didn't speak French. This frustrated the northern chap, as he wasn't speaking French. Part of the problem was him asking for 'egges' when the woman knew them as 'eyren'. Caxton wrote: 'What should a man these days write: egges or eyren?'"

Perry took a sip of water before continuing.

"Hence, Caxton standardized the English language by printing almost everything in the London dialect. While spoken English initially retained its regional characteristics, a standardized printed English enabled a formal education to be useful anywhere. From Caxton's time onward, regardless of location, educated people were able to discuss complex ideas without hindrance, be it business, politics, medicine, art, or anything else. It was an ever-growing influence too, which saw the variations in spoken English also gradually diminish."

"Exactly," said Marston.

"How fascinating," said Imelda.

"Yes, very much so," enthused Major Tipton. "Imagine the confusion of a cavalry officer having to give an order to someone who speaks in a different dialect."

Marston guffawed. "Yes, your poor cavalry officer might give an order for a gin and tonic and be served ginger beer!"

While Perry's anecdote was well received, and Marston was largely ignored, little conversation flowed throughout the main course and dessert.

It was later that David Marston addressed Kate.

"Mrs Forbes, do you and Lady Jane still believe it wasn't an accident?"

It was an awkward question, especially with Dr Evans present.

"Is that a subject for the dinner table?" she asked.

"You're sleuths. What's your next move?"

Kate's late husband, Henry, had been a judge who often recounted courtroom tales across the dinner table. But she couldn't take David Marston seriously.

"It's not a game," she told him.

"From what I hear, you've supposedly solved cases the police couldn't. I'm interested, that's all. General theory and all that."

Kate took a moment. As much as the mood at the table was clearly against the theory of murder, nobody attempted to shut Marston down.

"Well," she said, "*generally* speaking, it's a matter of working out who had the opportunity to commit the crime. Then there's the means used and the question of whether a suspect had the capacity to use those means. Then there's the motive. Why kill someone? And why now?"

Jane took over.

"You cannot look at an event in isolation. You must also consider the context."

"Absolutely," said Kate, glancing at Imelda and deciding it was time to drop the pleasantries. "There may be important information that's deliberately held back by someone, sometimes for innocent reasons."

Marston laughed.

"The truth is this, ladies. If it were really murder, I would have identified the killer by now. It's a process of intelligent elimination, you see."

This provoked all into looking at those around them.

Marston continued. "Jasper knew Eliza better than most. And we certainly have some context there. Obviously, I'm not questioning the doctor's opinion – far from it! But in the name of general theory, if we were looking at opportunity... Major Tipton was quickly at the scene."

"What?"

Marston backed off.

"I mean... did you see anything suspicious?"

"No, of course not!"

"Really!" said Lady Alsop. "This has gone far enough. Our dear friend the doctor is with us."

"It's all right, Imelda," said Dr Evans.

"No, it's not all right, Richard. You've declared it a tragic accident. Let that be an end to it."

David Marston smirked.

"Let's be kind to Jane. I'm sure she didn't mean to stir things up like this."

All stared in Jane's direction.

"Something didn't feel right," she said. "I'm not a doctor though."

Kate felt sorry for her niece. Indeed, she felt the urge to leap in to protect her.

So be it!

"It's my fault," said Kate. "I've come to trust Jane's instincts. She has a sharp mind and, working alongside Scotland Yard's finest, she's solved some tricky cases. If she says something seems wrong, I'll back her up one hundred percent."

She hoped it would see Marston off.

It didn't.

"Ladies, ladies… honestly, I admire your spirit. Giving minor assistance to a Scotland Yard detective is the duty of all. The fact is any fool can arrive at the truth if they poke their nose into it sufficiently. I've done exactly that on this occasion and can reassure everyone that there's nothing in it."

Perry spoke up.

"I'm glad to hear it, Mr Marston. Just remember this. I've seen Kate and Jane in action. There's nothing minor in the way they've assisted the police."

Kate was fed up with the whole business.

"I'll get on to Chief Inspector Ridley of Scotland Yard in the morning. I spoke to him earlier and he was very interested in the case. I think I'll ask him to visit the mortuary and examine the body to see if the rusty iron bar Jane discovered matches the wound, even if the rust was washed away. Perhaps this will finally end all the speculation. I'm sure the chief inspector will support the doctor's opinion that it was an accident."

Major Tipton snorted. "Richard Evans is an exemplary doctor. He'll agree to that proposal in a heartbeat… won't you, Richard?"

All looked to Dr Evans.

But he could only stare at the table in front of him.

"Richard?" prompted Imelda.

The doctor raised his head and sighed.

"It wasn't an accident."

Most of the guests let out a collective gasp.

"I knew it!" said David Marston. "It's as clear as day when you think about it."

But no one was listening to him. All were waiting for Dr Evans to continue.

"Are you absolutely sure, doctor?" said Jonathan Deerhurst.

"Yes, I am. Eliza Cole's death was no accident. She was murdered by my son, Jasper."

There were more gasps around the table.

Even David Marston was speechless.

Major Tipton stood up.

"Doctor, you must stay here tonight. Your son too. The police will want to speak with you both."

David Marston looked put out.

"Um… the doctor was due to run me home later."

"You should stay too," said Imelda. "We all must."

Marston still looked troubled.

"Is there a room spare?"

"Yes, there's a spare staff room in the attic, David."

Kate almost smiled. It was good to see Marston have his style cramped. Unfortunately, the situation was too serious for light-hearted comments.

Just then Dr Evans stood up.

"Jasper and I will need some things for the morning. I'll drive home now. I shouldn't be more than an hour. David, I suggest you telephone your mother so that she has your things ready when I pass by."

Twenty-One

With all at the table rising to their feet, Lady Alsop requested that Dr Evans tell them everything before he left for home.

The doctor seemed to have trouble expressing himself, but Kate urged him to be courageous, however difficult the moment.

Dr Evans gave a little nod.

"I confronted my son before dinner. You see, I learned that Eliza Cole had ended her relationship with Jasper. I told him... I said... you must try to save the situation. He did his duty and went to see her... to persuade her... and she must have angered him. I'm sure her death came in the heat of the moment."

Major Tipton huffed.

"I don't think the doctor is the only one who should explain himself. Deerhurst, will you accompany me? It's time we got our hands on Jasper."

125

"He was using a spare room earlier," said Mrs Glessing.

The two men left the room.

Miss Sophie Pearce seems uncomfortable without having Mr Deerhurst present.

"Should we ladies withdraw?" she suggested.

"Not just yet," said Imelda. "I think we all need to see what Jasper has to say for himself before I call the police."

"Well," said Marston, "before you call the police, I'll call Mummy to put some things together for me."

A brief awkwardness ensued where some resumed their seats and others went out onto the terrace to take the air, even though the evening was chilly.

It wasn't long before Tipton and Deerhurst returned though.

"He's gone," said the major.

"We checked the front," said Deerhurst. "There are no cars missing so he won't have got far."

"I hope he hasn't done anything rash," said Perry.

"I'm heading for home then," said the doctor. "I'll be back as soon as possible."

As Dr Evans left them, Kate knew she wasn't alone in wondering if the doctor and his son were involved in some kind of conspiracy.

A few moments later, Lady Alsop was in her late husband's study making a call to the police in Eastbourne, with most of the guests at the door listening. She explained the situation to a duty constable who worked for the borough constabulary but who would contact the East

Sussex chaps. He knew their man Sergeant Nixon would want none to leave the house. As for a search party, nobody would be interested in traipsing through the countryside in the dark.

After the call, the men decided to take brandy and cigars in the sitting room.

Kate stopped Jonathan Deerhurst for a quiet word though.

"You said you knew the name of the killer."

"Yes, Jasper Evans. I was right."

Kate smiled sadly and let him go. She wondered. Was that it?

She was unable to follow Jane and Imelda to the drawing room though, due to Mrs Glessing summoning her aside.

"Imelda had her jewels stolen. At least, I thought so."

Kate frowned.

"Why are you telling me now?"

"I'm wondering if Jasper is the thief."

"Jasper? I see. What exactly happened to alert you to a theft?"

"Earlier today, I took Imelda's jewel box from the drawer to assist her. She tried to stop me, but I opened it."

"Are you in the habit of helping her?"

"We're old friends above all else. Yesterday, she took a couple of pieces out herself. The jewels were there then."

"So, a theft, and yet she refused to call the police."

"Yes."

"Even when you pointed out the jewels were missing?"

"Well, it was more that she looked stumped. Then later, she decided it was all a mistake and that the jewels were in safe keeping elsewhere."

"But you don't believe her."

Unusually, Mrs Glessing paused before speaking.

"Imelda has known Jasper since he was a boy. Perhaps she wanted to let him put things right. But now…? Honestly, I don't know what to believe."

Kate thought about it. The theft was recent. But was it related to the death of Eliza Cole?

"Before we attended the scene of Eliza's death, we saw Lady Alsop crying."

Mrs Glessing donned a pained expression.

"The poor woman has been in turmoil over something for a few days. Changing her mind this way and that. Possibly, we don't need to look beyond Archie Hammond's advances. She was comfortable with Major Tipton, you know. But there was little progress."

"And now there has been some?"

"I believe so. Imelda told Major Tipton not to pry. That certainly put him in his place. Oh, it's good to be able to talk with a like-minded woman, Kate. It's one thing to be starved of juicy information, but quite another to have no one to discuss it with."

"Well… Antonia… perhaps we'd better get along to the drawing room or we'll come under suspicion."

Mrs Glessing smiled. "Righto."

A few moments later, they joined Imelda, Jane and Sophie Pearce in the drawing room where a worried-looking Connie served them coffee before retiring for the night.

Kate needed some honesty from Imelda regarding what was troubling her but couldn't think how to raise it without causing upset or even annoyance.

Meanwhile, Antonia Glessing began chatting about weddings, with selected details from a few she had attended over the years.

Kate wasn't fooled. Mrs Glessing would have an angle. Clearly, she wanted to draw Jane, or possibly Kate herself on future plans. It was a surprise then that Imelda was the one to take the bait.

"I do feel it might be time to at least think about the future," she began. "It's been three years, and I've become frozen. All those thousands of books are Edgar's. I couldn't throw anything out. You know, having Perry here is timely. I do want a slimmed down, accessible library, but… I suppose it will also represent something. A move forward. A new outlook." She glanced at Antonia Glessing. "And, of course, our local libraries and schools will benefit."

Kate smiled.

"You must do what's right for you, Imelda. No one else can know your heart, so you mustn't let anyone influence your future because it might suit them more than you."

Kate followed that up with a glance at Mrs Glessing, who she believed to be jealous of her friend's prospects.

"When did you first fall in love, Jane?" said Mrs Glessing, proving yet again her innate ability to be intrusive.

"Oh… well…" faltered Jane.

"Come on, it's just a bit of fun. I think we're in need of it. Perhaps Miss Pearce will tell us?"

Miss Pearce looked shocked, but Jane leapt in, clearly to protect her.

"Aunt Kate, did I ever tell you about Albert Lawrence? He lived in the village."

Kate tried to recall the name but drew a blank.

"I don't remember you mentioning him."

"We were inseparable for a whole summer. I was hoping we'd end up getting married."

Kate was surprised.

"What stopped you?"

"I was nine, Albert was ten."

"Ah."

"Not long after, his family moved abroad."

"Ah, all hope dashed."

"The next time I saw him was at a charity function after the War. I wondered how it might be between us when we spoke. There was no spark though. We had nothing in common at all."

"Oh well."

Before Mrs Glessing could pursue her agenda further, Kate stepped in.

"How about a different game? Where's the most interesting place you've ever visited? Antonia, how about you start us off? We can finish with Jane because she's been to see the Pyramids!"

It was another forty minutes before the ladies went to join the men in the sitting room.

On entering, Kate smiled at Perry. Mrs Glessing did likewise.

Understandably, conversation remained stilted, with events still bearing down on them all. Miss Pearce did her best to engage another guest in idle chit-chat, although Kate suspected it was a mistake for her to choose David Marston.

"I understand you work in Eastbourne, Mr Marston. A junior manager at a paint retailer…?"

"A junior manager with *significant* prospects. I have people working under me. Well, one. A sixteen-year-old boy called Freddie Jameson who lacks my verve and vision."

Kate felt sorry for Freddie.

"What about you, Miss Pearce?" said Marston. "How many staff do you have assisting you?"

"Oh… none. There's only me, and I report directly to Mr Deerhurst."

Before Marston could respond, someone on the terrace opened the French doors.

The company turned as one to a young man wearing a dark two-piece suit.

"Jasper!" reacted Lady Alsop.

"I've been outside… under the stars. You know, thinking. Some of us can't eat, drink and be merry at a time like this. Have you forgotten Eliza already?"

"What are you talking about?" demanded David Marston. "You're the killer."

The impact of the accusation knocked Jasper Evans back a step.

"What's going on?" he demanded.

Deerhurst got in first.

"Eliza's death wasn't an accident."

"Says who?"

"Your father."

If the shock of the accusation had knocked him back, this latest revelation almost floored him.

"But… I'm no killer!"

Marston scoffed. "Sorry, old chap, but I suspected as much."

"This is nonsense!"

"It's not nonsense. It's been proven beyond all doubt."

A distraught Lady Alsop shook her head slowly.

"I'm afraid it's true, Jasper."

"Where's my father! I have to speak to him!"

"He drove off after dinner," said Major Tipton. "He said he would return…"

Kate wondered if it was too late in the evening to make a second call to Chief Inspector Ridley. She supposed under the circumstances it probably wasn't.

Just then, Brooke appeared from the hallway.

"Lady Alsop, a motorcar has pulled up at the front. I believe it's Dr Evans."

Twenty-Two

It was eight o'clock on Saturday morning, and the sun was rising in a clear sky. It would be a lovely day, which always made things feel a little better.

Kate hadn't slept well, particularly during the small hours, when the death of Eliza Cole had hung heavily over her attempts to drift off. Then there was the other reason for her bout of insomnia – the dream preceding it in which she was a guest at Perry and Antonia Glessing's wedding. Even in daylight, she shivered at the thought.

Certainly, sometime in the middle of the night, she stood at the window, peering into the darkness and wondering.

And now…

She thought of Perry and smiled.

When she first met Professor Nash, she beheld a man who was intelligent, pleasant, handsome, and a widower… not that she'd been interested in that sort of thing. Things had moved on since then though. It was the little things that made the difference – such as the time they pretended to be married to help Jane gain vital information. And the time they both wore Panama hats and each picked up the wrong one, so that Perry's sat high on his head like a comedy prop, while hers fell down over her eyes. She recalled Jane suggesting they should write their names in them. These weren't just daft moments – they were moments of connection, of being one of two.

She shook off the reverie. It was morning. The case was the thing.

She thought back to Dr Evans returning last night, and her subsequent call to Chief Inspector Ridley. He'd been intrigued to learn that Jasper Evans had murdered the woman who jilted him, and that the crime was initially covered up by the killer's father. Ridley's response had been short and direct. "Don't do anything until I get there!"

He would be leaving home about now and was due at Alsop House around lunchtime.

Kate went to Jane's room to find her up and raring to go. Neither wished to have breakfast downstairs with everyone else though, so took advantage of Connie's offer to bring coffee and toast with marmalade to Kate's room.

Connie also came in handy with certain information – namely, that no-one had left the house overnight and that David Marston had a bad neck from what he described as a rotten, horrible bed.

"Will that be all?" asked Connie.

Kate wondered.

"The thing is, Connie... we're in a tight spot. We suspected murder when no-one believed us. That has held up Justice, which I'm sure you'll agree should never happen. With that in mind, have you seen anything unusual here at any time over the past few days?"

"No, Ma'am. Nothing."

"Is there anything that struck you as even just a *little* unusual? Or perhaps something happened that wasn't a regular thing...?"

"Well..."

"Go on."

"A man in a car called yesterday morning. He drove Lady Alsop off and then brought her back. I don't know who he was but it's not a regular thing."

Kate smiled. "Do you know where they went?"

"No, but George Richards the footman was out front and thought he heard mention of Eastbourne."

"Thank you, Connie. It's probably perfectly innocent and unrelated to what happened, but we appreciate you telling us."

Once Connie had gone, they sat at the small table by the window and went over the events of the previous evening while enjoying their breakfast. Then there was the matter of the chief inspector's impending arrival. How would he react to events? Surely, he'd be happy with the doctor telling the truth about Eliza's death and naming his son as the killer. But were *they* happy with it?

Then there was the matter of the missing jewels. And what about the rivalry between Archie Hammond and Major Tipton? And why was Imelda crying that time? Had Hammond visited her in the sitting room? Had there been a tiff? Or some kind of ultimatum? Perhaps Major Tipton had been coming along?

And now there was the business of a strange man driving Imelda to Eastbourne and then bringing her back.

After breakfast, they left Kate's room to find David Marston lurking on the landing.

"Good morning, ladies! Fear not, this should all be over soon enough. It's what we call an open and shut case."

Kate smiled stoically.

"If you say so."

Not that he was listening to Kate. His attention was on Jane.

"There's a wonderful alternative to all this gallivanting about," he told her. "A man and a woman have a higher purpose, you know."

Jane smiled in the same way Kate had.

"Well, if you'll excuse us…"

"Shall I tell you something you don't know?" he said.

Kate doubted he had anything useful to impart.

"Please do."

"The police have just arrived," he said, at which he turned with a flourish and headed for the stairs.

Kate could only wonder why there was never a sharp pointy spear handy when you needed one.

"Right," said Jane. "We'll have to show them the cufflink and the crowbar."

Kate agreed. "It's a pity the chief inspector won't get here for a while, but yes, let's give the local police a bit of help."

Twenty-Three

Bright sunshine flooded through two large sash windows to light up the morning room, which overlooked the grounds to the front of the house.

Gathered inside were Kate, Jane, Perry, Lady Alsop, Mrs Glessing, Jonathan Deerhurst, Sophie Pearce, David Marston, Major Peter Tipton, Archie Hammond, Brooke, Connie and the footman George Richards.

Also present were Sergeant Nixon and Constable Roberts. They had arrived from Eastbourne on an unwieldy motorcycle-sidecar combination.

"Thank you for being here," said the sergeant. "Is Jasper Evans with us?"

It quickly became apparent that he wasn't. Neither was his father.

"All right… as this is now a murder inquiry, I'm going to need statements from everyone who was here yesterday."

Kate nodded. "I spoke to Chief Inspector Ridley of Scotland Yard last night. Did he manage to contact you."

The sergeant seemed annoyed.

"Yes, he did. I informed him that the East Sussex Constabulary has men capable of carrying out a murder inquiry. They're barely fifteen miles away in Lewes."

"But he insisted on taking over?" asked David Marston.

The sergeant ignored him.

"So," said Kate, "you're in possession of all the information Jane and I gave him."

"Yes, but I'm in charge until he gets here, and I insist that you keep out of it. I cannot abide interfering busybodies."

Kate was disappointed.

"As you wish, Sergeant. We won't trouble you."

"Now, let's find Jasper Evans, shall we?"

Deerhurst and the major led the two policemen upstairs, where Jasper had spent the night.

They soon returned without him.

"He's gone missing," the sergeant muttered at the bottom of the stairs, where everyone had gathered like a flock of sheep.

"Not again," said Mrs Glessing.

Lady Alsop looked shaken.

"I'm sorry about this, Sergeant. He gave me his word he would stay and explain himself to you."

"Are any cars missing?"

Brooke went outside and quickly returned.

"None missing," he reported. "But I found Dr Evans."

Just then, Dr Evans came in through the front door.

"Thought I'd try a walk in the grounds to the front. Ah, Sergeant. I'll help in any way I can."

"The best thing you can do right now, Doctor, is tell me the whereabouts of your son."

"Is he not in his room?"

"No."

"Ah… no idea then. Sorry."

"Right," said Nixon. "Apprehending Jasper Evans is my priority. Chief Inspector Ridley will look into all other considerations when he gets here, so please don't leave the estate."

"What about our statements?" asked David Marston.

"Later," grunted the sergeant. He then turned to Lady Alsop. "If I might use your telephone? Among other things, I need to organize a search party."

"Absolutely, Sergeant."

With Nixon busy in Sir Edgar's study, Kate targeted the doctor. He seemed more distraught now than before. Perhaps it had finally sunk in.

"Doctor…?"

"I'll resign first thing Monday morning," he told her. "You were right the whole time. All I did was block justice."

She felt sorry for him.

"The library then," announced Perry. "I may as well crack on."

Mrs Glessing followed him.

Kate smiled ruefully but drew Jane aside for a private word.

"I'm wondering if we should speak with the sergeant again."

"About the missing jewels, Aunt? Or the cufflinks? There's also the murder weapon. It's a pity he doesn't want our help."

Kate felt the same way. Why rule out the possibility of others being useful?

"The missing jewels, Jane. It seems unlikely Imelda simply put them elsewhere. Then there's Jasper. He could still be the killer. We won't overlook that. But has Dr Evans encouraged his son to flee? Or is he himself the killer?"

"There's plenty to consider," said Jane.

They waited ten minutes or so in the hallway for Sergeant Nixon to finish on the telephone.

"What is it, ladies?" he moaned on seeing them at the door. "I'm in the middle of organizing a manhunt."

Kate proffered the cufflink.

"We found this at the scene of the murder."

Nixon eyed it suspiciously before putting it in his breast pocket.

"You can explain it later. Right now, I have other priorities."

With that, he departed.

"We didn't mention the jewels, Jane."

"No, but our investigation must continue at least until Chief Inspector Ridley gets here."

"I'm ready. What's our next move?"

"We need to talk to Imelda."

As it was, Lady Alsop had returned to her room. This was no longer a barrier to Kate and Jane though.

When Kate knocked on her door, Imelda answered.

"Come in, Connie. I need that tea."

Kate opened the door and stepped into the room with Jane.

It was a large ante room that led to a second chamber, which would be the bedroom. This ante room looked comfy with a small green Chesterfield settee and a mahogany writing table where Imelda was seated. She looked up from a magazine as they entered, seemingly preoccupied – which was no surprise.

"How can I help?"

"Apologies for barging in," said Kate. "We just want to make sure the wrong man isn't hanged for murder."

Imelda was shocked.

"I'm sure none of us wants that."

"We believe your jewels have gone missing."

"Who told you that? Oh, I can guess. No, it's a misunderstanding, that's all."

"Are they important to you?"

"Yes… it's a ruby set. There's a tiara, necklace, earrings, brooch, bracelet and so on. It was a gift from Edgar."

"Is Archie Hammond staying long?" asked Jane.

The suddenness of the question had Imelda off-balance.

"Yes… it would seem so. He's family."

"And what of Major Tipton?"

Imelda looked distinctly uncomfortable.

"The major's an old friend. He fusses over me, that's all. He's a good man when you get to know him."

Connie appeared at the door with a pot of tea on a tray. At this, Imelda complained of a headache and a need to be alone.

"Put the tea on the table, Connie, then show them out, would you."

Twenty-Four

Kate and Jane entered the sitting room to think. It hadn't gone well with Imelda, and they needed to find another way forward.

"How many ways might jewels go missing, Jane?"

"Not too many, Aunt. They could be stolen, or you might put them in the wrong drawer. Or you might take them to Eastbourne."

"Yes, Eastbourne."

"That would be a very delicate matter to bring up, Aunt. I'd suggest we set it aside unless we have to rely on it."

Kate noticed Major Tipton on the terrace. He was talking to his valet, Mr Stamford.

"How about some fresh air?"

Before Jane could respond, Kate led the way outside.

"Major… Mr Stamford… we've just come from Lady Alsop. She has a headache."

"I'm not surprised," said the major. "The sooner the police capture Jasper Evans, the sooner we'll all be able to return to normal."

"Assuming Jasper is the killer," said Jane.

Tipton raised an eyebrow.

"What makes you say that?"

"Aunt Kate and I are going over the other possibilities. It doesn't hurt to be sure."

"Yes, well, I suppose you have a point."

"Have you said where you were before the incident?"

"Me? I'm sure I have. I went to my room."

"Did anyone see you?"

Tipton seemed unnerved.

"Stamford here must have seen me."

Before Stamford could speak, Kate cut him off.

"Mr Stamford was by the stream asking Billy about fishing. He wouldn't be able to vouch for you, Major."

"Well then… I'm not sure whether anyone saw me. I'm also not sure where you're going with this. Is there a reason for you to be poking your noses in?"

"Perhaps that's what led to Eliza's death – poking her nose in somewhere it wasn't wanted."

"Just what are you insinuating?"

"Nothing, Major Tipton," reassured Jane. "Is it fair to say you have Lady Alsop's interests at heart?"

"What of it?"

"Are you advising her on investments?"

The major baulked at that.

"Certainly not. Any advice I've given Lady Alsop is of a general nature."

"It's your area though, isn't it? You know someone in the City."

"I've taken an interest since I retired, that's all."

Kate attempted to take over, but the major waved a dismissive hand in front of her.

"I've nothing more to say."

He stepped into the sitting room, pulling the doors shut.

Kate addressed Stamford.

"Would you say the major was acting strangely before the murder?"

"I'm sorry, ladies, but I don't recognize your authority. It's also as plain as day that the police have their man – assuming they can catch him."

"We understand your loyalty…"

"I need to check the major's car for something."

They watched him scuttle away on a doubtless false errand.

"Jane, if Jasper Evans didn't kill Eliza, then what kind of motive would someone else have? Is this about an investment? Did Eliza learn something she wasn't meant to? Or are we just fishing and hoping for a bite?"

"Sometimes it's all any of us can do, Aunt Kate."

They strolled along to the next set of French doors. These were closed but through the glass they observed

Archie Hammond in the drawing room on a sofa smoking a cigarette.

They went in.

"Ladies... hello."

"I wonder if you can help us," said Kate. "We're not convinced the police are going after the right suspect."

"You think Jasper Evans is innocent?"

"There's an old phrase about leaving no stone unturned. You were in the library at the time of Eliza's death."

Hammond stubbed his cigarette into an ashtray.

"It's horrible to think I was reading dull documents while a murder was taking place. I hope the police are swift in catching the killer, whoever it might be."

"I'm sure we all hope that."

Hammond pushed his glasses up his nose.

"Sergeant Nixon assures us that good reliable police work is all we need. Perhaps you ladies should step aside...?"

"You told us you work in the City of London," said Kate.

"Yes, that's right."

"Advising on investments?"

"Investments? No, I'm in insurance. We provide cover for commercial buildings, factories and so on."

"Ryder Crown Insurance?" asked Jane.

"Yes, that's right."

"I saw it on the heading of your papers when you were in the library."

"You're observant."

"Do you provide cover for houses... such as Alsop House, for example."

"No, it's purely on the commercial side. Big contracts only. I hold a senior position, you see."

"I'd imagine it's a competitive business."

"Very much so – and clients can be short on loyalty."

"I can imagine.

Kate cut in. "Is there a rivalry between you and Major Tipton regarding Lady Alsop?"

"What? I've no idea what you're talking about. And I certainly wouldn't compromise Lady Alsop in discussing it."

"Absolutely," acknowledged Kate. "You were keen to be here for the competition weekend. Was that a ruse?"

"Certainly not!"

Hammond rose to his feet and bade them good morning before heading off into the hallway.

"What's the opposite of the Midas touch, Jane?"

Just then, Brooke popped his head around the door.

"Ah... can I get you some refreshment, ladies?"

"No thank you, Mr Brooke."

"Then... um..."

He entered the room with a troubled expression.

"What is it, Mr Brooke?" asked Kate.

"I'm sorry, but I overheard some of what you said. I know I shouldn't divulge information, but seeing as there's been a murder…"

"Whatever it is, Mr Brooke, you must get it off your chest."

"Yes, well… on Wednesday, Mr Webster and Billy were putting the first of the competition fences in place. Mr Hammond was watching from the terrace and asked me what they were doing. I told him and … well… he was surprised to learn of a competition being held at the weekend."

"Very interesting," said Jane.

"Do you think it's important?"

"Possibly."

"Ah well." Brooke had the look of a man who wished he'd not said anything.

Jane cottoned on and offered a warm smile.

"Mr Brooke, every scrap of information has the potential to be important. It just takes time for the pieces to fall into place, that's all. Sometimes, they never do. What else can you tell us about Mr Hammond?"

"Well… not much. He's no trouble at all as a guest, although I haven't had much to do with him. He definitely doesn't like any fuss. He goes up to his room last thing at night and comes down first thing in the morning for kippers, toast and coffee. That's about it."

"Thanks," said Jane. "We very much appreciate your help."

Looking a little happier, Brooke left them.

"Shall we see what Perry's up to?" said Kate. "He might have shaken off the delightful Mrs Glessing and learned something useful."

Twenty-Five

Kate and Jane entered the library to find Perry Nash minus Mrs Glessing. Kate smiled, but Perry merely sighed as he picked up a tatty volume.

"My heart isn't in this, Kate. Not after all that's gone on."

She sympathized.

"I know, but I'm sure you can find a few books in here and upstairs to give away to local libraries."

"I'm pretending upstairs doesn't exist, Kate."

"I know, but if you clear enough space down here…"

"…then it might be safe to try upstairs again. You're right, of course. There must be a few volumes upstairs I could put into the spaces I create down here. All that dust though…"

"Concentrate on this room first."

"I am, Kate. I haven't dared go back upstairs again."

"Imelda appreciates what you're doing, even if you started it purely as a subterfuge."

She turned to Jane who was admiring the painting on the wall.

"Jane?"

"Hmm…?"

"We were going to ask Perry if he's learned anything."

"Oh… yes. Have you, Professor?"

"No, sorry. I'm wondering though – if Chief Inspector Ridley were here, what would he do?"

"He would listen to us," said Kate. "Then he would speak to everyone, visit the crime scene, and no doubt search Eliza's room."

Jane smiled.

"Perhaps we could speed things along for him."

Perry frowned.

"Search Eliza's room without permission, you mean?"

"What if Jasper isn't the killer? What if the real killer is in the house? What if there's incriminating evidence in Eliza's room? Might it not occur to the killer to break in and remove it?"

"The door might be locked," said Perry.

"It isn't," said Jane. "I tried it earlier."

"Well… I suppose by breaking in first, it could be argued that we'd be safeguarding the chances of the police catching the real killer."

"Exactly," said Jane. "Could we borrow you?"

Perry put down the volume he'd been holding.

"You mean shenanigans."

"We do."

"Come on then."

The three made their way upstairs and were soon outside Eliza's room.

"This is easy," said Perry – just before a door opened at the far end of the hallway, forcing them to flee into Kate's room.

Kate stared at the professor.

"You were saying…?"

"Um… is the coast clear?" he asked Jane.

"I can't see who it is… but they've gone the other way. It must have been one of the staff. They'll have gone down the servants' stairs at the far end."

Just to be sure, the trio waited a few moments longer before emerging into the hallway and returning to Eliza's room.

"We need a lookout, Professor," whispered Jane. "Give us a knock if anyone comes along."

"Will do."

Kate disliked the business of poking around in other people's things, but she also understood the need for action.

Once inside, Jane pushed the door to and looked around the room. She then addressed a small cream chest of drawers, where it was evident that things had already been disturbed.

"Someone's beaten us to it, Aunt."

"That's not exactly ideal," said Kate.

Jane sifted carefully through the top drawer.

"The killer was no doubt looking for anything incriminating. They won't have taken anything they didn't need to though. Having anything of Eliza's on them would be a risk."

"I agree, Jane. Protecting one's neck from the gallows tends to promote caution."

Jane removed an open envelope from the middle drawer. There was a note inside it.

"It's signed by 'J'…"

"If the killer left it behind, it can't be important. J for Jasper, perhaps? Or J for Jonathan? What does it say?"

Jane studied it.

"It refers to a spring ball both Eliza and 'J' plan to attend. Let's hang on to it until the chief inspector gets here."

Perry knocked. Then they heard him engaging someone with an obscure historical point relating to medicine.

Kate guessed the interloper would be Dr Evans. Not that she had to wait to find out. Jane opened the door and said hello to him, following it with an explanation that they were searching Eliza's belongings but had been beaten to it by the killer.

The doctor seemed in no mood to challenge them.

"I wonder how Sergeant Nixon is getting on?" he mused.

"Perhaps we'll hear something soon," said Kate, although she had no idea why that might be the case.

The doctor headed off, leaving them to consider their next move.

"I think I'll go back to the library," said Perry. "Let me know if you need me."

Now they were a duo again.

"What do you think, Jane?"

"How about we have a word with Jasper Evans."

Kate raised an eyebrow.

"Aren't you forgetting something? Jasper has gone missing."

But Jane simply gave her aunt an enigmatic smile.

Twenty-Six

Kate and Jane headed away from the terrace and across the grounds towards the woods.

Jane pointed in the general direction.

"It's along the stream through there. It's an old trail, so it avoids the lower lying parts to stay passable most of the time. The stream twists and turns though, so we might lose track of it."

As far as Kate was concerned, the trouble with old trails through ancient woods was the lack of use. This inevitably led to unmanaged overgrowth and difficulty in getting anywhere.

Hence her frustration once they were in the woods and had to retrace their steps a few times.

They pressed on though, in the knowledge that they were probably going the right way and that the stream, which had meandered away, might meander back again.

That aside, Kate found it a pleasant experience, with dappled sunshine filtering through the trees and birds chattering above them.

"Ah…" said Jane. "Water to our right."

They now followed the stream for a few hundred feet, where it led to a significant feature.

"Recognize it, Aunt?"

"The bridge in the painting."

"The lane this side of the bridge forms an estate boundary," explained Jane. "The lane on the other side leads to a road between Lower Fincham and the coast."

It didn't take long to spot the fugitive Jasper Evans just short of the bridge. He was standing on a shallow bank beside a fallen tree trunk that Kate thought would make an ideal waterside seat.

"He's acting very suspiciously," she observed.

"So are we, Aunt."

"Yes, well… I must admit, I was worried he'd be miles away by now."

They approached, although he was looking the other way and had yet to see them.

Jane called out to him.

"Jasper?"

He turned and smiled.

"Jane, Mrs Forbes. How did you find me?"

"You left a clue in the library."

It took a moment for Jasper to catch on.

"Ah, my painting."

"Yes, although it was still a guess on our part," said Jane. "We felt if you were guilty, you'd be out of the county by now. But if you weren't, you'd just need somewhere you could think straight. Somewhere quiet and not too far."

"Most insightful, Jane."

"Your visits to Five Oaks go back a long way," said Kate. "I can imagine this place captured your artist's eye at an early age."

Jasper nodded.

"It has a special quality. The way the light changes in a thousand ways. I intended to paint it at least a dozen times, but I only did the one painting – a summer's morning. Lady Alsop loved it. I knew then that I wanted to be an artist."

"How old were you?" asked Kate.

"Seventeen. Now look at me, a dozen years later and out of luck. Unless you can help me…?"

Kate picked up on the irony. Jasper had told them not to question an experienced doctor. Now he was hoping they *would*.

"You might be off the hook for Eliza," said Kate.

"Oh?"

"Assuming you wrote this, that is." Jane read out the note signed by J. "I was pleased to learn you'll be at Five Oaks. I'm even more pleased to learn that we'll both be attending the Halton Spring Ball in May."

Kate hoped this might lift a weight from his shoulders, but Jasper shook his head.

"I never wrote it."

Kate sighed.

"I wonder who did?"

"Deerhurst, perhaps?"

Jane tucked the note away.

"Yes, Jonathan would be the other likely candidate. Did you know he was friendly with Eliza?"

"No, I didn't. Nor did I kill her. You seem to know how to investigate these things. Please find the real killer. I have no faith in the police."

Kate wasn't sure. Was he lying to them?

He clearly read their silence as doubt.

"Eliza and I were together, but she broke it off yesterday. She met someone else a few weeks ago – Jonathan Deerhurst, it would seem. The argument with my father was about me going to Eliza and trying to change her mind. I did go to see her, but she was certain of her decision and I respected her wishes."

"Your father assumed you lured her to the stables, had a fight, and killed her."

"Yes, but I didn't go to the stables. I wish I had. I might have saved her."

Kate considered it. Had this been a crime of passion? A hot-headed reaction? It couldn't be ruled out. But if Jasper wasn't the killer? Then who?

"Jonathan Deerhurst was planning to leave. And then he decided to stay – but only after we brought up the possibility of murder."

"That might be something," said Jasper. "The killer would be wary of leaving early and drawing attention to themselves. Leaving with everyone else after I'm arrested though… that would help them get away with it."

"Do you think Jonathan's the killer?" asked Jane.

"No, of course not. I mean… I don't know what to think. I'm just concerned that Sergeant Nixon will take one look at me and believe he's found the killer."

"You mustn't think like that," said Kate. "Sergeant Nixon couldn't find an elephant in a railway carriage."

"You're all under arrest!"

It was Sergeant Nixon coming through the bushes.

Kate smiled as best she could.

"Sergeant, what a splendid sight you are!"

"Really? All I heard was something about an elephant."

"Oh, relating to a different Sergeant Nixon serving in Africa."

"I'm not interested, Mrs Forbes. I arrived back at the house to see if Chief Inspector Ridley had left any messages for me, and I saw you leaving."

"And you followed us…?"

"Yes, because I knew you were up to something. I had no idea it would be assisting a man fleeing justice, but there it is."

"I'm no killer, Sergeant," Jasper protested as a constable came to handcuff him.

"Save your breath for the court, Mr Evans."

Kate was now very worried.

"Please remember, Sergeant, if Jasper's telling the truth, he'll be hanged for a murder committed by someone else."

"I'll bear it in mind, Mrs Forbes."

"You'd better have this," said Jane, handing over the note. "We thought it might exonerate Jasper, but it doesn't."

"You can put it with the cufflink," said Kate with an unconvincing smile.

Twenty-Seven

For twenty minutes, Kate and Jane were held under a mild form of house arrest in the drawing room, which included toasted buns and coffee. The rest of the household was banned from entering, which meant Perry couldn't hang about in the hallway.

Although the French doors were closed, the sash window was open an inch at the bottom, meaning the Oxford Professor of History could speak to them through the gap, thereby circumventing the strict police ban.

"The sergeant's still on the phone," he advised.

Perry had been sneaking into the house via the dining room to gather information. To Kate, he was a brilliant academic and a lovely man, but a terrible spy.

Just then, nearby voices in the hallway were followed by a knock and Sergeant Nixon entering. Perry had to duck down.

"Any news?" asked Kate.

"Never you mind, Mrs Forbes. I'm only letting you and Lady Jane go on the strict understanding that you stay out of it. It's a police matter and we have no room for amateurs poking their noses in."

"Yes, Sergeant. We understand."

"You're free to go too, Professor," said Nixon.

Perry's head popped into view at the window.

"Thank you, Sergeant. I'm sure Mrs Forbes and Lady Jane have the greatest respect for the forces of law and order, as do I."

Nixon sighed. "I accept you ladies were only trying to find Jasper Evans. And I'm grateful for the evidence you've provided. But, please, let that be an end to it."

He headed back into the hallway, closing the door behind him.

"What will you do now?" Perry asked through the window.

Kate opened the French doors to let herself and Jane onto the terrace.

"No idea," she said.

"Well, you know where I'll be – should you need me again."

They watched him go in through the library's French doors to enter the realm of books and dust.

"Atchoo!" was the last they heard from him before they strolled into the grounds.

"I think I can put some of it together, Aunt, but not enough to prove anything beyond all doubt."

Kate considered it.

"Should we mention Imelda's Eastbourne trip to Sergeant Nixon?"

"Right now, she'd tell him it's a personal matter unrelated to him holding Jasper Evans in a police cell."

"Fair enough. What about having a word with Jonathan Deerhurst?"

"You mean ignore the sergeant's instructions to stay out of police matters."

"Not at all, Jane. Jonathan is Lady Alsop's godson. It's our duty as friends to see how he's bearing up under the strain."

Jane smiled.

"Aunt Kate, you have a heart of gold."

They found Jonathan Deerhurst in the morning room reading a newspaper. Although the sun had moved away, the room was ideal for anyone wishing to sit alone.

He looked up as they entered.

"Ladies…?"

"We found a note among Eliza's things," said Kate.

"Oh?"

"We wondered if it was from you."

She explained its contents, and the fact it was signed by 'J' – which seemed to annoy him.

"What were you doing in Eliza's room?"

"Following in the footsteps of the killer, who got there first but failed to see the note as meaningful."

Deerhurst gave the matter some thought before answering.

"Yes, all right, I wrote it. I'd seen Eliza at previous Alsop horse weekends, but I didn't get to know her better until a recent function in London."

Kate sympathized.

"Did you keep it quiet because of Jasper Evans?"

"Yes... he thought he was going to marry her. You must understand that Eliza didn't choose me over him until last weekend. I mean she could have telephoned him or written to him, but she wanted to do the proper thing by telling him face-to-face at the first opportunity. She worked in London; he works in Eastbourne – but she knew they'd both be taking Friday off work to be here. Of course, I was to remain in the background."

"Until the Halton Spring Ball?" prompted Jane.

"Yes, as far as Jasper was concerned, he would hear that Eliza bumped into me at the ball and we got along from then on. Personally, I wasn't too worried about Jasper, but it's what Eliza wanted."

"Have you told this to the police?"

"The sergeant had his hands full with the search. I'll speak with him soon enough. Listen... I'm glad you pushed for a proper outcome. Had you not applied pressure, this might have been swept under the rug."

"We're still not sure Jasper killed Eliza," said Jane.

Jonanthan seemed surprised.

"Really? You don't suspect me, do you?"

"When we first suggested it might not be an accident, you decided to stay on."

Jonathan nodded. "You mean if I were the killer, I wouldn't want to draw attention to myself by leaving early."

"Just so," said Kate.

"We mentioned the killer beating us to Eliza's room," said Jane. "We also mentioned the note being deemed by the killer to be unimportant."

"Yes…?"

"It's just occurred to me that the killer might not have overlooked it."

"Ah," said Jonathan. "You mean the killer might have actually placed it there just before you showed up."

Kate was a little taken aback by this revelation.

Jane continued. "I hope Eliza has more notes from you in the same vein."

Jonathan smiled sadly. "At least four. I'm sure if you tell the police, they'll get to Eliza's home to confirm it long before I have a chance to fabricate and plant anything."

"That's good to know," said Jane. "The question is who else knew you were seeing Eliza?"

"Only Miss Pearce."

Kate was intrigued.

"Did Miss Pearce know you were sending notes?"

"Yes, she posted them for me."

"Well, thanks, Jonathan," said Jane. "We'll leave you in peace." Although, as they reached the door, she turned once more. "Um… Miss Pearce? Does she always accompany you to this kind of event?"

"Not usually, no. Friday was a normal working day for her. She has a small office at my house. She could have worked from there as usual. That said, I'm putting together a consortium of investors for a proposition I have in mind. Miss Pearce is compiling a prospectus, which requires my input. Then again, I told her I wouldn't be doing much with it on Friday and that she needn't come with me."

The investor comment had Kate's attention, but she chose not to show it.

"Miss Pearce could have worked in the office then?"

"Had she chosen to stay in London and have an easy day of it, then good for her. She was keen to be here though, which I might say is typical of her loyalty and professionalism."

"Do you run a company?" asked Jane.

"No, no… I have a sizeable network of contacts and do business from my Knightsbridge home, my club in Pall Mall, and my estate in Surrey. It's the way my father worked, and I see no reason to change it."

"I suppose the list of investors is confidential," said Kate.

"Absolutely."

"Would Lady Alsop's name be on it?"

"Well… as I just said, the list is private. But I don't see any harm in saying that Imelda's name isn't on it."

"You're quite sure?"

"Ah… you mean a killer would lie? I can assure you, Mrs Forbes, I'm no killer and no liar."

The ladies thanked him and closed the door. They only took a few steps though.

"Is it me, or has Miss Pearce been acting oddly?" whispered Kate.

"Something's not right," agreed Jane. "She lied about that phone call. She also lied about discussing fashions with Eliza. And now we can ask – why is she here?"

Kate was beginning to find Miss Pearce's connection to events ever more suspicious.

"Is she an obsessive type, Jane? One who has hidden feelings for her employer?"

"It's possible. Jealousy can be a powerful motive."

"Perhaps she resented Eliza being a rival. Perhaps she tried to warn her off and things got out of hand."

"I think she's in the drawing room, Aunt. Let's ask her."

Twenty-Eight

On entering the drawing room, Kate and Jane found a wire-bound notebook open on the side table. While a chair had been pulled up to it, there was no sign of Miss Pearce.

"We probably shouldn't look at that," said Kate as she moved closer with an interest in something written at the top of an otherwise blank page. "It looks like…"

She squinted.

"Strand 1254. Miss Alice Cosgrove. If I'm not mistaken, that's a London telephone number."

"It is," agreed Jane.

Sophie Pearce entered from the hallway.

"Oh…" she uttered as Kate stepped away from the side table.

"Miss Pearce," said Jane. "There you are."

"I went up to my room for something. How can I help?"

"There are a couple of things bothering us."

"Such as…?"

Sophie Pearce was clearly suspicious of their intentions.

"You've known the Deerhurst family a good while."

"Yes, I think I mentioned it earlier. I started working for them during the War when Mr Deerhurst Senior's aide joined the army."

"You stayed on after the War though."

"Yes, Mr Deerhurst Senior's original aide survived the War, thankfully, but decided to continue with an army career. I believe he's a captain now. As for me, I enjoyed my work and wanted to stay on."

Kate took over. "Would you say your keenness for the job has evolved into a strong sense of loyalty to the Deerhurst family?"

"Yes, it has, Mrs Forbes. That's not a crime, I hope."

"Absolutely not! It's admirable. Would it be fair to say you could have stayed in London yesterday and enjoyed a quiet time while Mr Deerhurst was preparing for the competition? He strikes me as a generous employer who would never begrudge a valued employee a little time to themselves."

"I had to be here."

"The work you're doing is urgent then?"

"Very much so."

Jane stepped in. "At the time of the murder, you were doing some paperwork in here."

"That's right."

"Did anyone see you?"

This shocked Sophie Pearce.

"I've no idea."

"Tell us about Jonathan and Eliza then."

"I don't know what you mean."

"Jonathan has already admitted to a growing friendship with Eliza."

"I see. Well… I can't see how raking over Eliza's private life helps anyone."

"Miss Pearce," said Kate. "How did you feel when Dr Evans identified his son as the killer?"

"What?"

"How did you feel?"

"I… what exactly are you implying?"

"Do you have feelings for Jonathan?"

"I refute that!"

"You made a telephone call."

"You must stop! The police have their man."

"We're not so sure."

"You are not the proper authority!"

"Indeed, we're not," said Jane. "The proper authority has taken Jasper to a police cell in Eastbourne. No doubt, he'll appear before a local magistrate on Monday to establish if there's sufficient evidence to send him for trial at the Old Bailey in London. I don't need to remind you that an Old Bailey judge has the power to send Jasper to the gallows."

Sophie Pearce looked sick with worry.

"It sounds like your only interest is to replace a guilty man with an innocent woman. Now please leave me alone or I'll summon Mr Deerhurst."

It was plain that Miss Pearce's words were final, so Kate and Jane thanked her and withdrew into the hallway.

"What do you think?" said Jane in a low voice.

"I think she's lying about not making a phone call," replied Kate. "What do *you* think?"

"I think we should call the number in her notebook."

"Strand 1254?"

"That's the one."

Jane was soon on the telephone in Sir Edgar's study asking the operator to put her through to the number in London.

"Oh hello… yes… Saturday, yes, of course, but… I see… yes… right… so, if I said the name Miss Alice Cosgrove…?"

While Jane spoke, Kate reminded herself that they should offer Imelda something for any calls they were making.

"Yes, Cosgrove, that's right… it would relate to Miss Sophie Pearce…"

A few moments later, Jane put the receiver down.

"It's Saturday, Aunt."

"I know, Jane."

"The number belongs to a staff hire agency. They're normally closed at the weekend, but there's a nice young chap in the office catching up on paperwork. He's been off with a heavy cold."

"There's a lot of it about, Jane. He's recovered then…?"

"Yes, he was well enough to tell me that Miss Alice Cosgrove is on their books and had an interview lined up for Monday at the Deerhurst household. Except, Miss Pearce has cancelled it. Understandably, he wouldn't divulge any further information."

"Quite right – but I'm none the wiser, Jane. It sounds like we've taken a wrong turn."

Jane glanced at her watch.

"We have an hour or so before the chief inspector gets here. How about we use it wisely?"

"Yes, well… a game of chess?"

"Always a good idea, Aunt Kate, but how about we pop down to the pub instead?"

"The pub?"

"Yes, we could take the professor with us."

Something occurred to Kate.

"This wouldn't have anything to do with Mr Webster, would it?"

Jane smiled.

"It might."

Twenty-Nine

Jane was at the wheel of her four-seater Triumph Super Seven, driving them along a sunny country lane to the Royal Oak pub in Lower Fincham.

"It's a treat to get away from that library for a bit!" said Perry from the back seat.

"It certainly is," agreed Kate from the passenger seat up front alongside Jane. In truth, she was enjoying a short break from the unrelenting questioning of suspects.

"I take it we're not going to the pub to relax though," guessed the professor.

"That's optional," said Jane. "But remember – Brian Webster gave a false account of his whereabouts at the time of the murder. He said he went to the stables from his cottage, but we know he came from the wrong direction for that to be likely. He did however come from the right direction if he'd been to the nearest pub."

"And let's not forget he smelled of beer," said Kate.

On reaching the heart of the village, Jane brought the car to a halt outside the Royal Oak.

"Right," she said. "If Mr Webster was here at the time of the murder, he can't be our killer. What we don't want is his friends giving him a false alibi."

"We can't let them know we're sleuths then," said Perry. "We'll have to blend in."

"Yes, blend in…" echoed Kate with a modicum of concern.

"Besides," said Perry, "I reckon I've earned an orange squash after all that dust."

"Orange squash?" said Kate with more concern than just seconds earlier. "What happened to *blending in*?"

"How do you mean?"

"Well, hereabouts, men would normally drink pints of beer."

"Oh, but I don't like drinking beer in the daytime."

Kate puffed out her cheeks.

"Just order a small one and pretend to sip it. Jane and I will do likewise with a small sherry."

Outside the pub, at an old wooden table, an elderly chap was sitting alone enjoying his pipe in the sunshine. He looked up as they climbed out of the car.

"Good afternoon," said Kate, noting that he was nursing the last of a small glass of beer.

"And you too, Missus!" he replied.

"Blend in…" Perry muttered to himself before pushing the door open.

The interior was surprisingly bright, and the pub clearly didn't just sell beer, wine and spirits – as evidenced by a display of general groceries.

A few men were beside the bar and speaking in low voices. They fell silent on witnessing the fresh arrivals.

"Ah, my dear landlord," said an undercover Professor Peregrine Nash. "I'm as thirsty as a desiccated rattlesnake. Give me a half pint of strong ale, and let's have some sherry for the gals."

Kate looked askance at him. Hopefully, they would now begin the business of blending in. But Perry had more to say.

"Anyone know a chap called Brian Webster?"

Kate exchanged a look with Jane.

"A good man!" exclaimed Jane hurriedly. "Mr Webster, I mean."

No response came.

Meanwhile, the landlord served their drinks and beheld his new customers.

"Terrible business at Five Oaks," he said.

"Oh yes," said Kate. "A terrible business."

"Why do you ask about Brian?" said a man standing at the bar.

"No reason," said Perry. "Lady Jane was just making the point that he's a good man."

Kate cringed while Perry took a sip of his beer.

"He is a good man," said the landlord. "A good and trusted man. I reminded the police of it when they came knocking here this morning. I also reminded them that Brian was in here yesterday at the time of the…well, the murder."

"Shush there," came a call from the corner, where a couple of men were playing dominoes. "They could be from the newspapers."

"All the better," said the landlord. "No harm in protecting Brian. He was drinking with Ronnie, wasn't he? No crime in that."

Perry held his beer glass up to the light to examine it with a degree of suspicion.

"Ronnie?" asked Kate.

"He's sitting outside."

"Ah," said Perry: "What's his preferred tipple?"

"That'll be whisky."

"Give me a double, would you?" said Perry, placing his beer glass and money down on the counter. "And keep the change."

"Thank you very much, sir."

A few moments later, they went outside, where Professor Nash approached the old chap.

"Would you be Ronnie?"

Kate looked around at the complete lack of alternatives while the old chap looked at them with a distrustful eye.

"Yes…?"

Perry set the double whisky down in front of him.

"Have a drink on us."

"Well, I must say that's very generous, Mr…?"

"Call me Nasher."

Nasher? Kate was learning more and more.

Ronnie took a sip.

"Ahh… just the ticket."

"I hear you know Brian Webster," said Nasher.

Ronnie took another sip.

"Nice whisky, this."

"Yes… um… regarding Brian Webster."

"You folks down from London?"

"No… well, Jane is."

"I don't hold with London. Too modern for me."

"Oh, but it's older than Lower Fincham! Did you know the Romans founded *Londinium* two thousand years ago? That's the square mile we know today as the City of London. It's mainly a financial district now – what we call The City…"

"What's that got to do with Brian?" interrupted Ronnie.

"Ah, yes, Brian…"

"Um, Ronnie?" said Jane. "Are you still working?"

"Yes, I work. For a bit longer anyhow. Everyone thinks I'm about to retire, but we'll see."

She then asked him where he worked.

Thirty

Arriving back at Alsop House, a refreshed Kate, Jane and undercover agent Nasher entered the vestibule satisfied that Brian Webster was in the clear.

Jane was saying how ruling Jonathan and Mr Webster out meant they were getting closer to identifying the real killer. She might have added that they were still a long way off, but a noise just out of sight in the hallway caught their attention.

"Hello?" said Kate. "Anyone there?"

By the time they looked, whoever it was had gone.

"We'll wait until the chief inspector arrives then take it from there," said Jane.

"In the meantime," said Perry, "let's see if we can find a sandwich."

In the dining room, an informal buffet had been laid out for lunch. The others had already eaten and were out on the terrace, leaving Kate, Jane and Perry to tuck into a sandwich at the table.

While they ate, David Marston was outside telling all something unexpected.

"Yes, I guarantee it. Jane will soon be naming the killer."

Kate almost choked on her bread and cheddar.

Marston meanwhile continued. "It's not Deerhurst or Webster, and I'd assume it's not Jasper either, otherwise why bother. No, Jane is just waiting for the detective from Scotland Yard to get here, then she'll reveal the name."

Perry paused between bites.

"I'm not convinced it's sensible to announce things like that." He leaned closer to Kate. "I'm sure he's a fool."

Kate couldn't argue with that.

Just then, David Marston came in from the terrace.

"I see our resident spies have returned."

Kate put her sandwich down.

"You had a thing for Eliza a while ago, but she rejected you."

"I beg your pardon?"

"Did you overhear her breaking up with Jasper? Did you believe it offered you a second chance?"

He laughed it off.

"Mrs Forbes… do you know I have an aunt who gives me advice. Mind you, she's hopelessly old-fashioned. If you disagree with her, you get a hefty swipe with her handbag."

Jane stepped in before Kate could consider the viability of what she'd just heard.

"David, where were you at the time of Eliza's death?"

"Hey! You're barking up the wrong tree, Jane. I know all about solving crimes. I once solved an important case."

"Oh?"

"It was at school. They still talk about it, I believe. The mystery of the store cupboard. Someone was stealing tools and supplies. My chums were stumped."

Kate had no interest but went along with it.

"What action did the school take?" she asked.

"We didn't tell anyone. We decided we'd solve the case ourselves. Basically, I hid in the cupboard overnight."

"Whose idea was that?"

"Most of the other boys."

"I see. Did you catch the thief?"

"Yes, it was the handyman. He wasn't stealing though. I followed him to a new store cupboard. He was transferring stuff, you see. It was a success though. Some of the boys thought we had a ghost, but I proved otherwise."

Kate smiled through gritted teeth.

"Well, Mr Marston, you really are the most... indefatigable man."

Perhaps her greatest fear was that one day, he might be put in charge of something important.

"Ladies," he said, "a killer needs a bitter mind in order to kill."

"Is that so?" said Kate.

"Take Major Tipton, for example. Once a proud cavalry officer but look at his poor regiment. All that glory and tradition. I'm sure you saw it in the newspapers – it's a bitter pill to have all that tradition swept aside by mechanization. Imagine the indignity of making the change from horse cavalry to the motor form."

"A sensible move," said Kate. "What's tradition when so much was learned at such cost during the Great War?"

"Ah… yes, my thoughts exactly. I'm just trying to show you how a poisoned mind comes about."

Jane, who had been quiet, returned to her earlier question.

"David, you still haven't said where were you at the time of Eliza's death."

"What?"

Marston seemed surprised to be dragged back to something he'd avoided. But he recovered quickly.

"Jane, listen… let me answer your questions over dinner in Eastbourne. I'm well known at all the top restaurants. Why, you and I would look as pretty as a picture. And I can afford the best."

"David…"

"Now I don't want you having ideas that your title and wealth have anything to do with it. Not when your beauty is the real talking point."

"You forgot to mention Jane's intelligence," said Kate. "She's very good at working people out."

"Ah, an intelligent woman always knows what's best for her."

He winked at them before leaving for the terrace once more.

Kate sighed.

"He's either completely stupid or a genius who's fooling us into ruling him out on account of him being utterly useless."

"It's a tough one," said Perry. "A killer though?"

Thirty-One

After a light lunch, Kate and Jane retired to Kate's room. It was an opportunity to discuss doing some pleasant things together in London during the coming spring and summer. Top of their list was a concert or two at the Royal Albert Hall, although this was quickly dislodged by shopping in Knightsbridge.

Ten minutes into their enjoyable chat, Kate spotted a note on the floor by the door.

"That's odd," she said as she went to get it.

It was a simple piece of paper, folded in half.

"It says, 'Meet me in the billiards room right away.' It's in block capitals, Jane… written to disguise any traits in the handwriting."

She handed it to her niece, who studied it.

"Unsigned, obviously. I doubt we'd be able to work out who wrote it."

"We'll hang on to it in case it's evidence," said Kate taking the note back and slipping it into her bag.

"The billiards room then," said Jane.

The ladies headed out of Kate's room and down the stairs. At the bottom, as they strode beneath the balustrade of the gallery, something caught Kate's eye. Jane was just ahead of her. An instinct had Kate push her niece in the back. Simultaneously, there was a crash and the sight of Jane sprawling across the floor.

Kate froze.

"Jane?"

The scene didn't make sense. Broken earthenware.... Hadn't there been a large pot up there...?

"Jane..." She reached down to the prone body. "Jane, please..."

A groan arose.

Then movement.

"Jane? Are you all right?"

"Ohh... I... Did something...?"

"Someone dropped a pot on you. I think it missed."

Very slowly, Jane sat up.

"Thanks for the shove, Aunt. I think you saved my life."

Kate seethed. "I will never forgive Marston for this. What kind of idiot tells everyone you're close to naming the killer!"

Jane groaned. "Unless he isn't stupid..."

Kate let that sink in.

"Of course… he might be behind the attempt!"

Others began to arrive, including Perry, who immediately hurried away to locate the doctor.

Meanwhile, Mrs Glessing assisted Jane, leaving Kate free to examine the stairs.

The balustrade ran across the gallery, which gave a clear view of anyone in the vestibule directly below it. It was inevitable that their route to the library meant coming down the stairs and passing under the balustrade. That meant whoever lifted the vase off its plinth and dropped it had been in a room nearby.

Kate mounted the stairs slowly, taking it all in. She cursed herself for not paying more attention. All her thoughts had been on the note and not on the immediate vicinity. She imagined a potential killer in one of the rooms, gloves donned, the door open a crack, an evil grin, a plan to match…

She reached the top of the stairs.

The nearest rooms appeared to be the best candidates. It seemed less likely that the perpetrator came from farther away.

She knocked on one of the nearest doors.

There was no answer.

She thought – if she entered, would the would-be killer be sitting on the end of the bed waiting for her?

No, by now, whoever it was wouldn't be anywhere near the scene of the crime.

She knocked again.

There was still no answer, although Brooke the butler appeared from the direction of the stairs.

"Mrs Forbes, is there any way I can help?"

"Whose room is this?"

"It's empty."

"Oh."

"It's near the stairs, so the occupant hears all the comings and goings. It's used as a last resort."

Kate tried the handle. The door opened.

There was a single bed and a small wardrobe. The sort of room to place an unexpected guest.

"It's not the room David Marston used last night, is it?"

"No, Mr Marston was in the attic. I don't think Lady Alsop wanted him to get ideas that he would ever be a welcome guest."

"He trades on the friendship of his parents then."

"Very much so."

A quick look around revealed nothing. That wasn't surprising though.

"This is serious, Mr Brooke. Is there anything you know that might help?"

"I really don't know what to make of anything."

Kate thought for a moment.

"Is there anything you can tell me about Lady Alsop over the past few days? She's been acting strangely."

Brooke looked horrified at the prospect of discussing his employer.

"All I can say is what's plain enough to any observer. Mr Hammond might have suggested to Lady Alsop that he's interested in her."

"I see. Yes…" It was hard to see how that had any bearing on events. Hammond or Tipton? Of course, it wasn't for her to say.

Kate and Brooke checked the other rooms without success. Then they went downstairs, where a small crowd watched as Dr Evans attended to Jane.

"A lucky escape," was his appraisal. "I'm glad you're all right."

"I feel responsible," said Major Tipton.

"How?" said Kate.

"Because I'm a fool. There was danger and I was unaware of it."

"I don't suppose there's any point in us visiting the billiards room," said Kate. "Clearly, a ruse."

"I think Lady Jane should rest," said the doctor.

"I'm fine," insisted Jane. "A bruise or two at most."

A commotion flared at the front door, where Brooke was letting someone in.

"Are you sure you're all right, Jane?" asked Kate.

"Absolutely… I… no… perhaps not. It must be a concussion. Only, I can see Harry as clear as day."

Kate wondered if Jane's concussion was contagious, because a lean, handsome chap with a friendly face, warm brown eyes, and swept-back brown hair had appeared.

"It *is* Harry!" she gasped.

"Good grief!" declared Harry Gibson. "Who's had a go

at Jane?"

"It's all right," said Kate, getting used to the idea that Harry was real. "She's just recovering."

While Harry went to Jane, Kate explained the situation to him, while also explaining to everyone else who Harry was.

"I spent too long in London!" he railed. "When Jane phoned me with news of the accident, I should have dropped everything and raced down here."

Kate was delighted. She could see that Harry was shocked though.

"You did the right thing in the end," she told him.

"Yes… to be absolutely honest, it was the phone call this morning from Professor Nash that sealed it."

"Perry?"

"Yes, he said 'the woman you love has had a great shock. Why are you still in London? Get down here right away.' Something along those lines…"

Kate's heart surged with feelings for Perry.

"I hope I wasn't too harsh," said Perry.

"Definitely not!" said Kate.

Harry smiled warmly. He and Jane then embraced.

"I have a theory," said David Marston.

Kate wasn't impressed.

"A theory, Mr Marston?"

"Yes… what if the vase was a distraction and that a real attempt will soon be made on me?"

Kate was tempted to enact it right away.

"Why on earth would you think that?" she said instead.

"Use your noddle, Mrs Forbes. The killer might have seen through me saying Jane was getting close. It would make sense that they believe it's me who's the real sleuth and that I'm onto them."

"Perhaps you should lock yourself in a spare room," said Kate.

"Ah, no, no… I, David Marston, have drawn out the real killer and saved the life of Jasper Evans. It should be much easier to solve the crime now."

Thirty-Two

Kate was with Perry in the sitting room, awaiting the arrival of Chief Inspector Ridley. Jane and Harry were outside on the sunny terrace taking the air. They looked happy together.

While Perry leafed a little too quickly through a newspaper, Kate thought about Antonia Glessing's point that the professor was already married to his work. Perhaps it was time for that little chat…

"Perry?"

He looked up from the paper.

"Hmm…?"

"Do you think a long-distance friendship is enough?"

He thought for a moment then put the paper down.

"You mean we need to address it."

"Yes."

"Otherwise… what's the point, you mean."

Kate almost gulped.

"Yes."

Brooke the butler entered with a grey-haired man in his mid-forties, standing tall in a dark blue suit with a white shirt and grey tie.

"Chief Inspector Ridley!" exclaimed Kate.

"Would you care for some refreshment, Chief Inspector?" asked Brooke.

"No, no… I'm fine, thank you." As usual, his voice was confident, with just a hint of a working-class background, while his manner was measured, as if haste would mean him missing something. "As soon as Lady Alsop is ready to see me, I'll be able to get on."

Brooke departed and Ridley turned to the two occupants.

"Always a pleasure to see you, Mrs Forbes, Professor Nash."

"Chief Inspector," said Kate. "It's good to see you too. We're so glad you're here."

"You came for the horse-riding competition then."

"Jane and I did, yes."

Perry folded his newspaper and set it aside.

"By a complete coincidence, I came to look at some books."

"I see," said Ridley with a smile. He knew of their friendship and was clearly pleased. "A happy quirk of fate that you're here at the same time then."

"Well…" said Perry. "There may have been a tiny degree of collaboration in arranging the coincidence."

Ridley laughed warmly and Kate knew they were with a friend.

"Ah," said the Scotland Yard man as Jane and Harry came in to join them. "It's good to see you both again."

Once greetings were exchanged, Kate set about bringing the chief inspector up to date, including the supposedly unrelated matter of Lady's Alsop's jewels. Most perturbing for Ridley, of course, was the news of the attempt on Jane's life.

"I'm hoping there was no lasting damage?"

"Alas, the pot couldn't be saved," said Jane with a reassuring smile, "but thanks to Aunt Kate giving me a hefty shove, I'm fine."

Ridley considered it.

"Whoever it was must have thought you were onto them. Are you?"

"Not yet," said Jane.

"Well, it wasn't Jasper Evans who attacked you. Thanks to Sergeant Nixon we have him in custody."

"Yes, he's an efficient policeman," said Kate.

"He is indeed," said Ridley. "I hear he captured a couple of ne'er-do-wells along with the fugitive. To be serious though, the attempt on Lady Jane doesn't mean Jasper Evans is innocent of Eliza Cole's murder."

"No indeed," agreed Kate. "We feel it could fall a couple of ways: Jasper being the killer and having a supporter try to muddy the waters. Or Eliza's killer is someone else who feared being named thanks to a foolish young man called David Marston. He blabbed about Jane's progress before the pot was dropped. There's also the matter of the cufflink we handed to the sergeant."

"Yes, you mentioned that on the phone."

"We've kept it secret. None of the guests or staff know about it."

"It might yet help us," said Jane. "Not with fingerprints though."

Kate concurred. "I found it in damp straw. Of course, if the killer dropped it, they would have got rid of the other one. But, as Jane says, it might still help us in a way we're not yet seeing."

"Yes, possibly," said Ridley. "You know, I didn't listen to you earlier. I'm listening now. Where was Jasper's father at the time of the second attack?"

"We can't say for sure," said Kate.

"Could he have committed the deed, got away, and come back again?"

"He could have used the servants' stairs to come down. It was a confused throng."

"Confused throngs are usually easy to blend in with, Mrs Forbes."

Brooke knocked and entered.

"Lady Alsop will be with you shortly, Chief Inspector."

"Thank you, Mr Brooke."

"Are you sure I can't tempt you to some tea or coffee?"

"Oh… why not. Tea, thank you."

"And a sandwich, perhaps. I see you were on route over the luncheon period."

"Mr Brooke… you've persuaded me. A sandwich would be wonderful, thanks."

"We have some rather good cheddar."

"Perfect."

Once Brooke had gone, Ridley made himself comfortable on the sofa.

"I'll have a word with Lady Alsop, then I'll interview those on Sergeant Nixon's list – apart from yourselves. If it's all right with you, I'll interview you afterwards. I'll be interested to see if you can add any insight to what I learn from the others."

"We should probably leave you to it," said Kate. "Unless you want us to sit in with you and Lady Alsop?"

"No thanks, Mrs Forbes. I'll get back to you in due course."

Kate, Jane, Perry and Harry bade him good day and withdrew to the sunny terrace.

"What do we think?" said Perry.

"I'm not sure," said Kate. "Chief Inspector Ridley is in charge now. He's a good man and a good detective. He'll get to the bottom of it."

"What if he doesn't?" said Harry.

"It wouldn't hurt us to go over what we know," said Jane. "There might be some detail we think of that could assist him."

"He's a good friend," said Kate. "He deserves our best efforts and full support, even though he's technically on Sergeant Nixon's side and not ours."

"How do we proceed?" asked Harry.

"We mustn't undermine the police," said Perry. "There's a still a possibility that Jasper Evans is the killer."

"But if he isn't…?"

It was apparent that they were being watched by Mrs Glessing from the library and by Major Tipton from the terrace by the dining room. Then Archie Hammond came out from the drawing room for a cigarette.

"Where shall we discuss it?" said Perry.

"Jane and I know just the place," said Kate.

Thirty-Three

Kate, Jane Perry and Harry followed the old trail through the woods.

"It's not far," said Kate.

They needed somewhere quiet to think things through. Somewhere they wouldn't be spied on or casually overheard.

As it was, while the matter of uncovering the killer's identity was uppermost in Kate's mind, something else occurred to her. It was how much she enjoyed walking through the woods with Perry. Obviously, any closeness was hampered by the presence of the younger generation, but she knew she wanted to spend more time with him. She was sure Jane felt the same way about Harry. She smiled as she recalled her own youth, when she believed only the young understood love.

"There's a bridge over the stream," she said. "Why don't you two try through there…"

As soon as Jane and Harry went off, Kate took Perry's hand.

Perry smiled. "You know, a chap and his lady could get quite close in the woods."

Kate agreed and so leaned in and kissed him.

Perry's eyes widened.

"I meant Harry and Jane."

"Ah."

Then Perry laughed and kissed her in return.

"Perhaps we should look for the bridge," she eventually suggested.

They strode onwards, with Perry whistling a jaunty tune and Kate feeling positive about the future.

"I'm so glad Harry came down," she said.

"Yes, at difficult times, it's good to have someone to lean on and confide in."

"And cuddle up to?"

"Oh definitely."

A call echoed through the woods. It was Harry.

"I think they've found it," said Perry.

They retraced their steps and headed the way Jane and Harry had taken. A few moments later, they reached the stream. Harry and Jane were waiting for them, hand in hand, by the fallen trunk on the bank.

The ladies soon claimed the trunk for seats while the men remained standing.

"What a lovely place," said Harry, taking in the scene.

Perry was staring towards the old stone bridge with a puzzled look on his face.

"This seems familiar somehow…"

"It's in a painting on the library wall," said Kate.

He looked around again and slowly nodded.

"So, this is where you found Jasper."

"Yes, it's a place he likes to visit."

"I can see why. It's so peaceful."

Harry swept his hair back. "I suppose the question now is – can we help him? That's assuming we *should* help him."

"I don't think the police will mind," said Perry. "They were close to investigating Jane's death at someone else's hand."

Both he and Harry glanced at Jane with a blend of concern and relief.

"We have the irrepressible David Marston to thank for that," said Kate. "That said, he may have flushed out the real killer. Then again, it might have been a ruse that allowed David to act against Jane without bringing suspicion upon himself."

"Ah," said Harry, his features registering this alternative way at looking at it.

"We can't decide if Marston is a fool or a genius," explained Kate. "He had a potential motive, in that Eliza rejected him once and may have rejected him a second time."

"He has quite the bloated opinion of himself," said Perry. "Does that make him a killer though?"

"What about the cufflink?" said Kate. "Dropped by a man… or a woman hoping we'd assume it was a man."

"I'm not sure that gets us anywhere," said Jane.

"What else do we have?" asked Harry.

"Jasper was in a police cell when Jane was attacked," said Perry. "But you heard Kate explain it to the chief inspector – what if a sympathizer was trying to weaken the case against him."

"Who would help him like that?"

"For a time, his father tried to cover up the murder."

Kate considered Dr Evans and his initial lie.

"He admitted to his deception though," she said.

"Perhaps he had to," said Perry. "A post-mortem examination and a Scotland Yard investigation would surely have uncovered his deceit."

"That's true enough," said Kate.

"Could it have been anyone else?" said Harry.

Kate shrugged.

"We're fairly sure it wasn't Jonathan Deerhurst… but that does leave the question of his secretary, Sophie Pearce. Did she kill Eliza in a jealous rage?"

"Hardly anyone can prove their innocence," said Perry. "Then again, they don't have to. It's up to the law to prove their guilt."

"We probably need to concentrate on plausible motives," said Harry.

"Agreed," said Kate.

"Major Tipton…?" suggested Perry. "His attention seems to be on Lady Alsop. What's really going on there? I mean can Lady Alsop trust him? Can *we* trust him?"

Kate wondered. "The major might simply be someone who has a heavy-handed way of showing that he cares for her."

Perry's shoulders slumped.

"I'm sure you're right, Kate. What about Archie Hammond?"

"Similar to Major Tipton," said Kate. "Archie takes a great interest in Imelda's wellbeing. That said, he's not a regular at Alsop House and I don't think he knew Eliza."

"What about if he was up to no good, and Eliza found out?"

"That's a suggestion that applies to almost any guest. That said, Jane says Archie Hammond lied about being in the library. It's almost certain he'd been with Lady Alsop and caused her a great deal of upset."

"Poor Imelda," said Perry.

"Yes, Imelda," said Kate. "There's the business of the missing jewels. Mrs Glessing assumed they had been stolen, but Imelda took a trip to Eastbourne. It's possible she was trying to raise money."

"That's not a crime," said Perry. "Five Oaks is in decline. Anyone can see that. She may have debts that need paying off."

"Do you know our biggest problem?" said Jane.

"What?" asked Harry.

"For motive, it always comes back to Jasper Evans. Eliza dumped him."

"But he wasn't responsible for a pot nearly killing you," said Harry.

"We're going round in circles," said Perry.

An impasse ensued in which Harry picked up some small twigs and threw them one at a time into the water, watching as they drifted away.

It was Kate who broke the silence.

"Perry stumbled across a Victorian author of numerous volumes on the Tudors."

"I've already admitted my jealousy," said Perry. "I wish I could find the time to write a series of books."

"You just need somewhere without all the distractions of Oxford," said Harry.

"In case you've forgotten, Harry, Oxford is my place of work."

"Of course, but… well… perhaps you'll retire one day."

"Perhaps."

"They make a fuss of senior professors retiring," said Harry, mainly for Kate's benefit. "A ceremonial role and a word up the line to Parliament and the King. Arise Sir Peregrine, sort of thing."

Perry frowned. "Yes, thank you, Harry. As I said, perhaps."

The company fell silent once more. And once more, Harry resumed throwing sticks into the glistening stream, while Kate wondered if they were out of their depth.

She also wondered about Perry receiving a knighthood at Buckingham Palace. He'd become Sir Peregrine Nash, and she would be Lady Nash. Assuming they ever got married.

Perry puffed out his cheeks. He seemed set to say something… something Kate hoped might prove illuminating. But he puffed out his cheeks a second time and thrust his hands into his trouser pockets.

"I'm famished," said Harry. "What time's tea?"

"Four o'clock," said Kate. "Can you hold out for another two hours?"

Harry warmed to Kate's gentle teasing.

"I'll manage, Mrs Forbes. I wonder what cake they serve?"

Kate gave a wry smile.

"I have it on good authority that it's chocolate."

"We are powerless to resist," said Perry.

Kate and Harry laughed. But their laughter soon faded. There was no overlooking the fact that solving the matter of Eliza Cole's murder appeared to be beyond them.

"We've tried our best," Kate told Jane – although her niece's attention was elsewhere.

Kate followed her gaze to the old stone bridge, over which a shepherdess and her collie were driving sheep. There was a bit of a hold up thanks to the bridge being too narrow to allow them all through at once.

"They get about," said Kate. "I'm sure it's the flock we saw yesterday when we drove through Lower Fincham."

"Looks like they need a bigger bridge," said Perry.

"Hmm," said Harry. "I'm only sorry I missed the trip to the pub."

"Perhaps we could go again," said Kate. "I mean Perry's practically a local."

"I could show Harry how well I work undercover."

Kate turned to see if Jane was enjoying the levity, but she wasn't. Jane looked troubled.

"One mistake, Aunt. That's all I ask."

"A mistake by the killer?"

"Yes… there must be something."

"Perhaps," said Kate, although she held out little hope of finding it.

Thirty-Four

Returning to the house via the terrace, they found Imelda and Mrs Glessing in the sitting room.

"Any sign of Chief Inspector Ridley?" asked Kate.

"He's on the telephone in Edgar's study," said Imelda.

"Thanks."

Kate and Jane headed off to join him, leaving Perry and Harry to keep the ladies busy.

Ridley nodded as they entered. He was sitting behind Sir Edgar's desk with the receiver to his ear.

"The operator's trying to put me through to London," he explained.

"How did you get on with Lady Alsop?" asked Kate.

"That's confidential – mainly because what we discussed isn't related to the Eliza Cole case."

Kate felt frustrated.

"I take it you're referring to the missing jewels?"

"Regarding that, Lady Alsop has assured me that no crime has been committed."

"Do you know the whereabouts of the jewels?"

"No, but her late husband was Sir Edgar Alsop, a man with connections. Unless I can find a link between Lady Alsop and the murder, I have no business chasing it."

"So, you've accepted her story?"

Ridley sighed.

"Occasionally, not everything is related."

"I agree," said Jane, "but what if, on this occasion, everything *is* related?"

"Absolutely," said Kate, "there's a possibility that Imelda Alsop's jewels and Eliza Cole's death are no more a coincidence than Peregrine Nash and myself being here at the same time."

But Ridley's attention returned to the phone.

"No…? Oh well, thanks for trying."

He put the receiver down.

"No answer in London. No matter. Now, I'll be very interested to hear your theories, but first I need to confront Jasper Evans with what I've learned so far."

"You've spoken to everyone here?" asked Jane.

"I have and it throws up some questions for the young man in custody. Once I've got some answers, you and I will sit down and go through what you've come up with so far. Unless you can name an alternative killer right away…?"

"No," said Jane. "Not at this moment."

"Right then," said Ridley, picking up the telephone again. "I need to make another call. An important one."

Kate and Jane acknowledged his intention but remained.

"You don't need to be here," he advised.

"Ah, is it the Commissioner of Police?" wondered Kate.

"No, my wife."

"Ah right. Give our regards to Mrs Ridley."

Ridley put the phone down again.

"Actually, I'll call her from the police station in Eastbourne."

They followed him along the hallway to the vestibule, where they encountered Imelda leaving the sitting room and heading for the stairs.

All nodded politely as she passed, while Ridley mentioned he'd be away for a while. Imelda merely smiled respectfully without stopping.

Kate and Jane followed Ridley out the front where his car was waiting. A constable was nearby looking bored, but on seeing the chief inspector he snapped to it and got behind the wheel.

"Ladies," said Ridley, "if you're thinking of questioning Lady Alsop, think again. The business Mrs Glessing thought might be of interest to the police was a simple misunderstanding."

They watched him get into the car.

"Chief Inspecter?" said Kate before he could close the door. "I think the idea that the missing jewels and the murder are unrelated has to be challenged more thoroughly."

"You mean put pressure on the widow of a Knight of the Realm? You do know her husband was a highly respected man?"

"We'll push gently. With your permission, of course."

Ridley sighed. And then he shrugged.

"All right. You've not let me down before. Let's hope my trust isn't misplaced this time around."

"It won't be."

Ridley closed the door and lowered the window.

"There's a telephone at the police station. Do not hesitate to call me if anything important crops up."

"Will do."

"Eastbourne, Constable," Ridley told the driver. He then sat back as the car pulled away, leaving Kate to second guess their plan.

"Jane? Are we doing the right thing?"

"I'm not sure, Aunt, but I think we'd regret not trying."

Thirty-Five

A few moments later, they knocked on Imelda's door.

"Come in."

"Sorry to disturb you again," said Kate, "but we have some urgent questions."

"I've already answered all the Chief Inspector's questions." She said it in a way that suggested there couldn't possibly be any other questions she need concern herself with.

"We hope to save an innocent life," said Kate, "but we're going to need your co-operation."

Lady Alsop sighed. "I have nothing to add."

Kate was disappointed. Here was someone whose privacy presented a barrier to Kate's most cherished cause – Justice.

"Sorry to pry, Imelda, but did you recently raise a substantial amount of money?"

"I beg your pardon?"

"A man visited. He drove you to Eastbourne."

"That's private."

Kate took the necessary leap.

"Was it to do with your jewels going missing?"

"I... don't know what you mean."

But the slight hesitation told Kate otherwise, and she was ready to press home her advantage.

"Antonia thought they'd been stolen."

"Antonia was wrong. They weren't stolen."

"Could we see them?"

"Really, this is too much. It has nothing to do with poor Eliza's tragic demise."

"Please... show us the jewels."

Imelda refused.

But Kate stood her ground.

"I hate to ask, but have you pawned them?"

Imelda's eyes widened but she said nothing.

"Imelda... did you put them in hock to raise money?"

Again, a determined silence.

Kate felt sorry for her. For a moment, she wondered why Imelda didn't just sell off her paintings to raise money, but then she supposed they weren't particularly special and that selling them would be an all-too-visible indicator of financial strain.

"The jewels," repeated Kate. "I urge you to co-operate."

"Mrs Forbes…" said Imelda with a heavy sigh. "Regarding my valuables, the police are not required to act when no crime has been reported."

"Lady Alsop…" said Kate, mirroring Imelda's tone. "If Jane and I believe it to be linked to a murder inquiry, then the police are very much required to act. It's essential that you tell the truth."

Once again, Imelda assured them that her little matter was unrelated to Eliza's tragic death.

"Then you leave us no choice," said Kate. "We'll advise Chief Inspector Ridley to send men to every pawnbroker in the south of England. They'll be asking about Lady Alsop needing to hock her jewels."

Lady Alsop's shoulders slumped as a deep shock took hold, but Kate couldn't afford to show mercy – not if she wished to save an innocent life.

"Imelda… the police would start in Eastbourne."

Lady Alsop was close to tears.

"This is so unfair."

"Imelda, we will not place anyone's reputation above the value of a human life. A young woman was murdered in your stables and an innocent man may hang for it. It's time you re-examined your priorities."

An impasse ensued while Lady Alsop no doubt considered her options.

"Very well," she finally said. "Sir Edgar bought the jewels for my thirtieth birthday. I now regret the whole business."

"Go on…"

"I'm short of funds. As you would expect, I've kept it quiet."

"You sold a horse you loved to a nearby stables."

"Pippa, yes. It broke my heart but I'm closing the Five Oaks stables. I just couldn't bear to see her there at the very end. She's not a competition horse, so there was no need for her to be here this weekend."

"Was this to be the final competition?"

"Yes. All that tradition… lost. The thing is, Edgar refused to face the facts. He would spend money we simply didn't have. For example, the house has electricity and telephones. He insisted on having it put in despite the expense and then he died leaving bills that were extremely difficult for me to pay."

Jane nodded. "The money you raised from the jewels… if you're using it to directly pay off debts, we'll leave you in peace. If the money was for something else though, you must confide in the Chief Inspector and allow him to act."

Imelda stared at the floor.

"I'm not sure I can."

"Please… Lady Alsop."

"I'll think about it."

There was a knock at the door.

"Come in," called Imelda.

It was Sophie Pearce.

"Is everything all right, Lady Alsop? I thought I heard raised voices."

"Everything is not all right, Miss Pearce, but I shall have to bear it."

"We'll leave you to it," said Kate.

She and Jane headed off to the landing, where they found Perry and Harry coming up the stairs.

"I thought I'd better take another look at the overspill," groaned the professor.

"We'll come with you," said Kate. "We can give you a little update. Not that we've achieved much."

They entered the overspill room, where Perry heaved a sigh before addressing a shelf crammed with books.

Jane meanwhile picked one up from the side table.

"The Empress of Watering Places," she said, reading the title. She put it down again and lifted the trunk's wicker lid.

Inside, she had a good rummage. Beneath the clothes, she found three small brushed-velvet boxes: one black, one midnight blue and one deep crimson. The first of these was empty. The other two contained cufflinks.

She showed the empty one to Kate.

"How interesting, Jane. If the killer was here, their fingerprints would be... lost under yours."

Kate studied the small box's covering.

"Not that brushed velvet offers usable prints."

She then studied the lid of the trunk.

"Nor wicker..."

Jane meanwhile was examining the inscription inside to cufflink case.

"It says 'Joseph Bell, Bespoke Jeweller, Eastbourne'…'"
She turned to Perry. "Professor, when were you last in this room?"

"Um… yesterday with you and Kate."

"What is it?" asked Harry.

"The sheep on the bridge," said Jane. "I did wonder about that."

"I don't understand," said Kate.

"The sheep, yes… we were looking for a way to use the cufflink we found at the stables. And now we have it."

"Do you know the killer?" asked Perry.

But Jane was already leaving the room.

Thirty-Six

As requested, those who were at Five Oaks at the time of the murder gathered on the sunny terrace at the rear of the house. For a moment, it reminded Kate of the previous day's gathering to draw the names of horses from a hat. But this would be far more serious than who might win a sweepstake.

At Jane's request, Chief Inspector Ridley had come straight back from Eastbourne, bringing Jasper Evans with him. He'd also brought along Sergeant Nixon, Constable Roberts and another constable called Ayre who brought a second police car.

Understandably, some of those gathered were muttering about the situation.

Although not all…

"Wonderful views," said Mrs Glessing. "It really is a lovely day."

David Marston harrumphed.

"No, Mrs Glessing, it's a horrible day."

"Too right," said Brian Webster. "I'd like to say it couldn't get any worse, but I've a feeling it's about to."

Kate kept an eye on Jane, who looked just fine after the attack. That said, Dr Evans was standing close to Jane's left, seemingly keen not to let his patient out of his sight. To Jane's right was Ridley.

Seated on dining chairs that had been brought outside were a handcuffed Jasper Evans, Kate, Lady Alsop, Mrs Glessing, and Sophie Pearce. The staff, the sergeant and the constables stood behind them.

The rest of the men stood to Jane's right. These were Perry Nash, Harry Gibson, Jonathan Deerhurst, Brian Webster, Archie Hammond and David Marston – all of whom bar Marston were wearing jackets and ties. Marston was in shirtsleeves, which were rolled up, suggesting he was ready for action.

"Why are we here?" he asked. "And more to the point, why is Jasper here?"

Jasper remained impassive, but Ridley nodded.

"I'd say the case against Jasper Evans is strong enough for an Old Bailey jury to find him guilty of murder. Be in no doubt, a guilty verdict would send him to the gallows."

Mrs Glessing blew her nose into a tissue.

"However…" said Ridley.

Kate noticed everyone's attention intensify.

"Would this 'however' relate to Major Tipton?" asked Marston. "I see he's gone missing."

"We'll come to that shortly," said the chief inspector. "The most important thing is to understand what happened yesterday, and why. Now, Lady Jane Scott has come up with an intriguing theory. That's why we're here."

He stepped back to give Jane the floor.

"Thank you, Chief Inspector. I'll try to keep this brief. I know some of you would prefer to be elsewhere but if you could bear with me, I'd like to offer an alternative explanation for what happened at the stables. One that points to the real killer."

"Yes, Major Tipton," said Marston.

Jane met his gaze then moved on.

"We discovered a private note in Eliza's room. It was signed by 'J'. The friendly tone of the message and the fact that Eliza had kept it – it surely exonerated Jasper Evans. However, Jasper was honest in refusing to claim authorship, even when it offered him a glimmer of hope."

She turned to the men.

"Jonathan Deerhurst, a gentleman of considerable standing and Godson of Lady Alsop recently met Eliza Cole at a function. He began to see her regularly from then on. Isn't that right, Mr Deerhurst."

A grim Jonathan Deerhurst nodded.

"Yes."

"And the note was from you."

"Yes."

Jane's focus switched to Sophie Pearce.

"The note suggests a happy arrangement between Jonathan and Eliza – one you, yourself, can confirm."

"Yes," said Sophie.

"You do understand that clearing Mr Deerhurst of suspicion has the effect of bringing you out of the shadows."

Sophie said nothing, so Jane continued.

"You've been acting strangely since Eliza's death."

"That's no surprise," said David Marston. "She has feelings for Deerhurst. Any fool can see it."

All turned to Sophie Pearce, whose face had turned a deep shade of red.

Thirty-Seven

Jane prompted Sophie Pearce.

"Miss Pearce, you made a telephone call on Friday afternoon…"

"Why are you interrogating me in front of all these people?"

Jane paused before addressing the complaint.

"Let me answer that in a moment. You made a phone call on Friday afternoon, which you later denied making. In that call, you mentioned a change of plan. Did that change of plan have repercussions, such as the cancellation of Miss Alice Cosgrove's interview?"

Sophie took a breath.

"How do you know about Miss Cosgrove…?"

"I had a chat with a chap at the agency. A job interview had been set up for Monday, but you cancelled it. In the light of events here, it's hardly surprising."

Sophie said nothing, so Jane continued.

"This would have been an interview for which job exactly, Miss Pearce?"

Sophie Pearce wouldn't say.

"Perhaps I can help you then," said Jane. "The interview was to find a replacement for yourself."

"No," said Jonathan Deerhurst.

Jane's focus remained on Miss Pearce.

"Am I right?"

Sophie swallowed drily before answering.

"Yes."

Jonathan looked confused but said nothing, while Jane continued with Sophie Pearce.

"Your loyalty to the Deerhurst family runs deep. It was always going to take quite something to make you look elsewhere. Who did you call on the phone?"

"It's private," she said.

"Private, yes – but it wasn't a call to an accomplice in a murderous scheme… and your professionalism rules out you sharing gossip with anyone. This person on the other end of the line… they would be very important to you."

Sophie gave the slightest nod but remained silent.

"Miss Pearce… Sophie… who were you calling?"

"I…" Whatever she'd had in mind, Sophie Pearce thought again. Her determined expression softened and gradually became one of resignation. "I was calling my fiancé."

Jonathan Deerhurst could barely contain himself.

"Fiancé, Miss Pearce?"

Sophie turned to him with a sad smile.

"I was going to tell you yesterday afternoon." She hesitated before continuing. "Mr Deerhurst... I'm so sorry to say... I'm leaving your employment. After all these years with your family... well, I've been dreading ending the wonderful professional relationship I've had with yourself and your father before you. My fiancé hasn't put any pressure on me, but I want to be by his side. He needs a personal assistant, and I've decided to take on the role. I'd hoped to find a suitable replacement to take over from me, which is why I'd arranged for us to interview Miss Cosgrove."

Deerhurst's stern features broke into a grin.

"Miss Pearce... Sophie... I'm delighted for you. It's wonderful news."

Sophie brightened.

"Thank you, Mr Deerhurst."

"I was wondering if something might be going on. I heard talk of Sir Ralph Devine being seen with you."

"That's him."

Jane smiled. "Congratulations on your engagement, Miss Pearce. I'm sure we *all* wish you the very best."

"Thank you."

"Is that where the fashion advice came in?"

"I thought I needed to be a little more creative, so I asked Eliza."

A moment of reflection passed before Jane spoke.

"I'd imagine you were hoping that Mr Deerhurst would be so happy with Eliza that he wouldn't miss your companionship quite so much."

"Yes... exactly that. I was going to hand Mr Deerhurst my one month's notice yesterday evening."

"But events overtook you."

"Yes."

"And so you telephoned the agency to cancel the interview and then made a call to Sir Ralph to let him know of the tragedy and the inevitable change of plan."

"I knew I needed to delay leaving Mr Deerhurst. Anything else would have been insensitive."

"It was a very caring thing to do," said Jane. "I hope you'll forgive me for bringing it all out. To answer your earlier question, I won't allow Eliza's killer room to whip up tales of secretive liars with hidden motives. A jury that isn't certain must acquit. That's why the truth is best out in the open. It's my intention to corner the killer with no way out."

"And you will!" said Kate – at which Marston piped up again.

"I'm right then. It was Major Tipton!"

"Mr Marston, please..." urged Ridley.

David Marston seemed pleased with himself.

"I'm right, aren't I. It's Tipton. I knew it all along. He's guilty and he's fled!"

Jane met his gaze. "All in good time."

"Why don't I take over from you…?"

"Kindly control yourself, Mr Marston," chided Ridley. "Lady Jane knows what she's doing."

"With respect, Chief Inspector, are you sure?"

"Quite sure, thank you."

"Only, I have a superior mind compared with the common man… or woman. Instead of guesswork, you'd do well to listen to my understanding of the case. You would learn precisely why Major Tipton is the killer."

Ridley turned to Jane.

"Lady Jane, if you'd care to continue."

"Perfect timing," said Jane. She was looking beyond them all to the open countryside beyond the oaks. "I said a quarter past. The army understands punctuality."

All were now turning to witness a distant horseback rider approaching.

"That's Major Tipton!" declared Brian Webster. "He's not riding Apollo though. That's Pippa!"

Lady Alsop seemed bewildered.

"I… I don't understand."

"Nor do I," said Webster.

"What's going on?" demanded Marston.

"Dashed if I know," said Mrs Glessing.

"You lied to us, Mr Webster," said Jane. "You gave us a false account of your whereabouts at the time of Eliza's death."

"Oh… but…"

"You told us you were at home, but you came from the wrong direction. Of course, it was the right direction for anyone coming back from the pub."

Webster was clearly worried.

"I was seeing a chap at the Royal Oak, that's all. It was just a bit of business, nothing more."

"You were meeting Ronnie there. You've been hoping to find a new job for some months without luck, and Ronnie is at an age when he might soon retire. He'd need to be replaced at the Bridge Way stables by someone with experience. Someone who can handle a dozen horses."

"Bridge Way stables?" asked Marston.

"It's where Pippa ended up. No, Mr Webster, you're not the killer."

Brian Webster seemed both relieved and concerned. While he was no killer, all now knew he had a wish to get away from Five Oaks, probably because he knew it would soon leave him high and dry.

Just then Stamford appeared around the side of the house.

"Mr Stamford?" asked Marston.

"I just got back from Bridge Way. I had to drive the major there as per Lady Jane's instructions. I'd better go and assist him."

As he stepped off the terrace to assist the freshly arrived major, Jane addressed them all.

"We learned the whereabouts of Lady Alsop's horse from a reliable source called Ronnie." She smiled at Brian

Webster. "Thankfully, Pippa was sold to a friendly stables' owner. It wasn't too difficult for Major Tipton to buy her back."

"I still don't understand," said Lady Alsop.

"Don't you worry," said Kate. "I'm sure everything is going to turn out just fine."

Jane resumed. "While Major Tipton and Mr Stamford settle Pippa in at the stables, could I please ask everyone else to go to the library."

"Why the library?" questioned Marston.

"Because that's where I'll be able to throw some light on what happened yesterday afternoon."

Thirty-Eight

It took a few minutes and more questions from David Marston, but with all eventually stationed around the sunny library, Jane stood in front of Jasper's painting.

With only one seat available, all had to stand – apart from Professor Nash, who declared feeling faint and so took the red leather chair.

Jane began.

"Wherever you were, at some point you heard either Billy reporting an accident, or someone else relaying the message. Eventually, we all arrived at the scene where Dr Evans declared Eliza's death an accident."

"But you didn't believe it," said Jonathan Deerhurst.

"My aunt, myself, and Professor Nash considered the alternative – and the truth eventually came out."

"Yes, at dinner," said Marston. "Even I was shocked. Fancy Dr Evans dobbing his own son in it."

"Yes," said Jane, "at first glance, Jasper seemed the most likely suspect."

"So why bring us here?"

"What better place to reveal a hidden story than in a library?"

She turned to Archie Hammond.

"Why are you looking at me?" he complained. "I hardly knew her."

"I mentioned a hidden story. It's a story of investing money for a sure-fire return. We first thought of Major Tipton and Jonathan Deerhurst, both openly acknowledge an interest in the subject. If we turn the pages of this hidden story though, we find it's you, Mr Hammond. You're the one arranging an investment deal for Lady Alsop."

"Who told you that?"

"Lady Alsop."

Imelda sighed. "Kate and Jane persuaded me to confide in them. Against all my beliefs…"

Jane continued.

"The investment amounts to purchasing shares in a small insurance company that is about to be taken over by a much bigger one. Once the proposed takeover is announced, the price of shares in the smaller company will soar. Obviously, buying those shares before the announcement would be a sure-fire way to make a lot of money very quickly. But to do that, you would need insider knowledge."

"What of it?" scoffed Hammond.

"You're with Ryder Crown Insurance, a sizeable company. They're supposedly secretly about to buy Lowther Prentiss Insurance, a much smaller company. During high tea yesterday afternoon, Aunt Kate overheard Lady Alsop in quiet conversation with Eliza Cole. Indeed, the closer my aunt got, the more intriguing it became."

Kate nodded. "I heard Lady Alsop's comment, that her investments were her own business… and Eliza telling her that being hasty might be unwise."

"I don't see where this is getting us," said Marston.

Jane sidestepped his criticism.

"Eliza wasn't killed for nothing. If Mr Hammond was up to something crooked, I was sure Chief Inspector Ridley would be able to use his powers to learn something of it."

"It's an invasion of privacy," said Hammond.

"I was being fair," said Jane. "If you're an honest man, the chief inspector would find nothing."

"What did you find?" Marston asked the Scotland Yard detective.

Ridley gently cleared his throat.

"As requested by Lady Jane, I made a telephone call to Ryder Crown Insurance. I got nowhere. It's Saturday afternoon. They close at lunchtime for the weekend."

Marston scoffed. "I could have told you that."

Ridley pressed on. "I contacted a colleague of mine, a senior officer in the City of London police force with extensive knowledge of City misdeeds. He had contact details for a senior partner at Ryder Crown relating to a previous matter. Anyway, I phoned this Ryder Crown chap at home, and he told me something disturbing."

"I can't think what," said Hammond. "It's a reputable firm."

Ridley eyed Hammond. "You're right. It is. But you're no longer part of it."

Hammond shrugged and checked his jacket buttons, which were fastened.

"What of it?"

Any annoyance Ridley felt was lost amid Lady Alsop's outburst.

"What on earth is going on, Archie?"

It took a moment for Ridley to calm the situation before continuing.

"A few months ago, Ryder Crown was due to buy Montrose Insurance, a failing firm, whose shares would shoot up once it became public knowledge. Anyone with insider knowledge of the deal would be able to buy shares in Montrose beforehand."

"Using insider knowledge is not a crime," said Archie Hammond.

"It should be!" exclaimed Major Tipton, entering through the French doors. "It's unfair on us honest investors!"

Ridley continued. "Mr Hammond, you never had a senior role with Ryder Crown. You barely rose up the ranks. When you learned of a proposed takeover, you needed to find out the name of the other firm before the news broke. You'd be able to buy ahead of the announcement at a low price then cash in. It didn't go according to plan though, did it."

"No comment," said Hammond.

"While using insider knowledge isn't illegal, breaking into your boss's office safe after hours is. The City of London Police arrested you. However, the firm decided that losing your job and the damage to your reputation was a sufficient punishment. Hence, criminal proceedings were halted."

Jane took over. "A few months later, with no job and no money, you came here with a fake takeover story to reel in Lady Alsop. Let's be clear. Royal Crown is a real company. Lowther Prentiss Insurance is real too."

"There you are then."

"But the takeover doesn't exist. You invented it. And yet Lady Alsop, looking to solve her financial problems, finally overcame her doubts yesterday afternoon and handed you a cheque for five hundred pounds."

"That's scandalous!" protested Mrs Glessing.

"The lowest of the low," seethed Major Tipton.

"She's an adult," said Hammond.

"Eliza suspected fraud," said Jane. "She challenged you."

"Nonsense."

"She challenged you and you murdered her."

Hammond let out a lengthy sigh.

"Lady Jane... you're forgetting something. I have an alibi. You. And your aunt. And the professor."

Marston threw up his hands.

"My goodness! Lady Jane is Mr Hammond's alibi...?"

Thirty-Nine

Jane gave the revelation a moment to circulate before addressing it.

"Your alibi, Mr Hammond…?"

"I was in this very room while that despicable act was taking place."

"Yes, apparently waiting for Professor Nash."

"That's right," insisted Hammond. "I was in here waiting for the professor. I knew Imelda was short of money, so I thought it would be handy if the professor and I were able to unearth a few valuable books for her to sell."

"While you waited, you read through some detailed contracts."

"Yes, exactly. You and Mrs Forbes can vouch for me – in a court of law, if necessary."

"Let me see… you were seated in the red leather chair. It looks quite comfortable."

"It is," confirmed Perry.

Jane smiled but it didn't last.

"Mr Hammond, how long were you seated in that chair reading documents?"

"At least fifteen minutes. As I said, the whole time the terrible act was happening elsewhere."

"You sat in that chair reading over contracts with small print. A thorough reading then."

"Yes, very thorough."

"You didn't get up at any point?"

"No, I didn't move from that seat. Just as I was finishing, you and your aunt came along. Then the alert came through about the accident. At least, at the time, we believed it to be an accident."

"It took a while to work it out," said Jane. "Just how we might dismantle your alibi."

Hammond's gaze dropped while he shook his head slowly. Kate hoped he was about to admit everything.

He then raised his eyes to Ridley.

"Chief Inspector, I insist you stop this nonsense. With respect, I believe Lady Jane Scott has lost all reason."

Ridley remained steadfast.

"Lady Jane, please continue."

Jane did so.

"What glorious weather. Isn't that right, Professor?"

Seated comfortably in the red chair, Perry seemed taken by surprise.

"What? Yes. Lovely."

Jane took some papers she had left on a shelf some time earlier and handed them to the professor.

"Could you read these for me."

"Yes, of course."

Perry Nash began to read.

Hammond huffed.

"What is this?"

"Yes, of course, it's not quite right," said Jane. "Professor, could you put the chair back where it was yesterday at precisely this time?"

Kate glanced at the clock. It was a quarter to five.

Perry moved the chair and sat down again. He had to squint though – the sun was low enough to shine through the French doors directly into his eyes.

"Feel free to read aloud, Professor."

Perry did so but he was immediately having some difficulty.

"It's actually quite problematic. Could I move the chair again?"

"No, sorry. Just read, please."

He began again but was clearly in some discomfort.

"Really, Jane, this is quite impossible."

"I agree. The question is this – would anyone sit there for fifteen minutes reading detailed contracts under those conditions? They would be blind. Mr Hammond wasn't affected by sunlight because he reached the library just before we did and had to jump into the seat and pretend to be finishing his work."

Lady Alsop looked relieved.

"Jane said she would throw some light on what happened – and she has." She turned to Hammond. "If you'd really been sitting there, you would have moved because of the sun."

"Yes… but…"

Jane concurred. "It's the thing I noticed when we entered the library yesterday afternoon – Mr Hammond sitting there, supposedly reading his paperwork, with the sun glinting off his glasses.

Hammond became furious.

"I have to say this is an outrage! A hideous, ghastly trap!"

"Yes, sorry about that," said Perry. "It's all my fault for moving things around. There are so many books…"

Ridley took over.

"Mr Hammond, you attempted to hide your movements at the time a murder took place."

"Be fair," said Marston. "At first we thought it was an accident."

Ridley frowned.

"A false alibi for an accident?"

"Mr Hammond knew it was murder," said Jane. "That's why he needed an alibi."

"Is it alright if I move this chair now?" asked Perry.

"Yes, of course," said Jane.

Perry did so and stepped away from it.

"Imelda, would you care for a seat?"

"Oh, but aren't you feeling unwell, Perry?"

"No, that was Jane's idea – a ruse to destroy Mr Hammond's alibi."

"This is all very clever," seethed Hammond. "Yes, I'm a conman. But Scotland Yard's finest will get no further with the business of murder. And neither will you, Lady Jane. Let's end this nonsense right away. You cannot prove I was at the stables. That's the real fact of the matter."

"Well," said Jane, "at least permit me to try."

Forty

Archie Hammond examined his fingernails, as if this were a more important use of his time. But Jane looked confident enough.

"You say I cannot prove you were at the stables."

Hammond looked up.

"Exactly that."

"It was the weekend of the Alsop Challenge Cup, and you were keen to be here. In your own words, you wouldn't have missed it for the world."

"That's right."

"It's not true though, is it? On Wednesday, Brian Webster and young Billy were putting up the first of the competition fences. You asked Mr Brooke what they were doing. When he explained, you were surprised that there was to be a competition this weekend."

Chief Inspector Ridley addressed the butler.

"You're prepared to state that in court, Mr Brooke?"

"Yes, Chief Inspector. It's the truth."

Jane's focus remained on Hammond.

"Admit it. You had no idea there was to be a horse-riding competition at Five Oaks."

Hammond seemed to consider its importance.

"Well… what does it matter. I have no interest in horses. So what?"

"You have no interest in horses, which meant you didn't know Eliza's preferred horse was Ariadne. It's how you came to put her body in the wrong stall."

Hammond reacted badly.

"You must be off your head, young lady!"

"Eliza planned to ride while the competition course was quiet. You followed her to the stables, and you killed her in the courtyard with an iron crowbar."

"No… no!"

"You had to act fast in placing the body. Unfortunately, you chose Max's stall."

"This is insane."

"You had a one-in-six chance of choosing the right stall and you lost your bet. Had you chosen Ariadne's stall, we'd never have suspected a crime."

"Gambling never pays," muttered Mrs Glessing.

Hammond waved a dismissive hand.

"I'll state my case once more. You cannot prove I was at the stables."

"We found a cufflink near the body."

While Jane showed off the cufflink and its box, Hammond gasped with fury.

"Anyone could have dropped that!"

"That's what I thought," said Jane, "until I saw a flock of sheep."

"What?"

"Sheep, Mr Hammond. A shepherdess was herding them across a bridge."

Hammond turned to Ridley.

"She's nuts!"

"We'll come back to the sheep," said Jane. "First, let's establish that you came to Alsop House on Wednesday and only intended to stay for a day or two."

"Not true."

"As you weren't interested in horses, we wondered if your extended stay might have been due to a romantic inclination towards Lady Alsop."

"Indeed!" exclaimed Major Tipton. "That's what I feared. On Wednesday, I came here for a brief visit, but I could see right away that something was wrong. I went home but I wasn't happy. So, I packed some clothes and returned within a couple of hours ready to see him off."

Jane took over. "For you, Mr Hammond, this was an unforeseen problem. Unforeseen, because you knew very little of Lady Alsop's life over the past few years. You certainly had no idea that she had an admirer in Major Tipton."

While Lady Alsop blushed, Jane continued.

"The major knew Lady Alsop was in turmoil. He wanted you to leave. Of course, you wanted *him* to leave. Anyone looking in would no doubt suspect a rivalry. I certainly failed to see it in its true light. Your false alibi in the library – I wondered if it was even that, an alibi. It seemed you might be attempting to avoid Major Tipton's ire at you upsetting Lady Alsop. But it wasn't that at all. Lady Alsop's discomfort *was* tied to you, Mr Hammond, but it had nothing to do with an affair of the heart. Lady Alsop needed money, and you had a surefire scheme."

Kate glanced at Imelda. She looked crestfallen.

But Jane wasn't finished.

"As it was, Lady Alsop didn't have the money to invest so had to find a way to raise it. It meant pawning jewels her late husband bought for her. She wouldn't tell anyone though. Not even her friend Antonia Glessing, or her admirer Major Tipton."

By now, Lady Alsop was crimson.

Jane continued. "A couple of days ago, Lady Alsop handed the jewels to a trusted and private pawnbroker in Eastbourne. A cheque for £500 was handed over which she could deposit at her bank. It all took time. She wouldn't deal in cash. She wanted a record of everything. For you, Mr Hammond, it meant you didn't dare leave Alsop House because you feared the major might persuade Lady Alsop to tell him what she was doing and advise her to run away from the deal. That's why you were at a horse weekend with no interest in it."

Hammond muttered something unpleasant about horses, which Jane ignored.

"Finally, Lady Alsop wrote you a cheque for £500 from her account this afternoon. Much to your disappointment, you watched her draw two very annoying parallel lines across it before handing it over. We all understand how a crossed cheque cannot be cashed and must go through the banking system. Your stay at Alsop House was being extended yet again. And any single moment you left Lady Alsop to Major Tipton was an opportunity for him to discover the deal and talk her into stopping the cheque."

Hammond huffed.

"You think you're a smart woman, Lady Jane, but you've failed to prove I killed Eliza. I do hope your friend from Scotland Yard reflects long and hard on trusting you again."

Jane continued regardless. "Eliza Cole worked out what you were up to. She suspected a scheme that would benefit one person only – you. She knew the real reason you were staying longer than you originally intended."

"This is all nonsense. I always intended to stay a whole week, horses or not."

"Not true. You only intended to be here for a day or two. Major Tipton's presence forced you to stay on, but you didn't bring enough clothes to last till the weekend."

"This is foolish drivel. You have nothing on me."

"On the contrary, there's a spare room where the overspill books are kept. Lady Alsop is only now getting around to having a proper clear-out. Books, collectibles, and clothes. Some of Sir Edgar's clothes were folded away in a wicker trunk. You learned of it."

"I didn't."

"Yesterday, Professor Nash placed a copy of *The Empress of Watering Places* on the lid of the trunk. It's a fascinating book about Eastbourne's seaside between 1752 and 1920. A short while ago, we found it on the table next to the trunk."

"It wasn't me," said the professor. "I didn't move it."

Jane nodded. "Mr Hammond, I was looking for a mistake you might have made. And there it was. No one goes into that room. Except someone did. Someone was clearly going into the trunk to borrow Sir Edgar's clothes. His cufflinks too. It's hardly a crime, and you certainly never came to Alsop House with the intention of murdering anyone, so why not help yourself? It's just that your helpful mistake in moving the book led me to an empty cufflink box. As I said, we found a cufflink at the scene of the crime."

Hammond appealed once more to Ridley.

"A book? Anyone could have moved it!"

"Well," said Jane, "perhaps fingerprints would help us there, but to prove what? That you entered a room? No, that wouldn't do at an Old Bailey trial. The cufflink though…"

"As I've already stated, anyone could have dropped it. I certainly don't have the other one."

Jane continued. "Can we prove the cufflink at the scene of the crime came from this little box? Yes, because the name of the bespoke jeweller is printed inside it. Joseph Bell of Eastbourne. I asked the Chief Inspector to check if he's still trading, and he is. All we need do is check if Mr Bell made and sold the cufflinks to Sir Edgar. I have complete confidence that he did."

"What?"

"It's quite simple, Mr Hammond. There are some good quality tailored white shirts in that trunk, along with the cufflinks that were in this box. No-one would blame you for borrowing them."

Marston piped up. "Sorry, Jane, but you really haven't nailed him. Not to my satisfaction, anyway."

Jane continued. "No? Then allow me to bring on the sheep."

Forty-One

Jane didn't hesitate.

"Archie Hammond presented himself as a successful man. He couldn't wear the same shirt over and over, especially with these warm, sunny days, and he wouldn't want the staff to know what he was up to. He certainly never allowed staff into his room. Of course, he could have returned to London to get more clothes, or gone to Eastbourne to buy some, but that carried the terrible risk of Major Tipton having a lengthy chat with Lady Alsop."

"The sheep?" prompted David Marston.

Jane smiled. "We watched a shepherdess and her collie taking a flock of sheep over the old stone bridge on the edge of the estate. Only, there was a woolly log-jam as not all the sheep could fit on the bridge at the same time. Professor Nash said they needed a bigger bridge, which made me think of something else that didn't fit. Mr Hammond, at dinner, it wasn't too hot. Your shirt collar was too tight. We also saw your shirt buttons under pressure, supposedly from too much cake. The sheep made me see it differently though. They told me that both the bridge and your shirts were too small."

"I… no…"

Jane pointed a finger. "Who makes your shirts, Mr Hammond? Sir Edgar's shirts were tailored by a chap in Eastbourne, but of course you told us you've never been to Eastbourne."

"Well…"

"You were borrowing things from Sir Edgar's trunk. Shirts… and cufflinks, one of which we found at the stables. Mr Hammond, I have placed you at the scene of the crime."

"I, um…"

Ridley stirred. "Mr Hammond, I'd like to see the tailor's label in your shirt."

"Label…?"

Hammond took a step towards the open French doors. And then another.

And then he grabbed a book and threw it at the approaching Constable Roberts.

"Hey!" cried Perry. "That's a Regency poetry anthology!"

Hammond headed for the terrace, but Harry stuck out a foot, which had the would-be fugitive stumbling and sprawling as the policeman caught up and grabbed his arm.

"Up you get…"

A defeated Archie Hammond rose under supervision, and brushed dust off his jacket.

Ridley stepped forward.

"Archibald Hammond, I'm arresting you for the murder of Eliza Cole."

But Archie Hammond wasn't at all interested in hearing it.

"I hate the Alsops. They should have helped me years ago!"

Lady Alsop shook her head.

"Poor Eliza. Why?"

"It was either her or me," sniffed Hammond.

"Explain!" demanded Ridley.

The killer visibly slumped.

"The information I gained from the break-in... I told a chap who I owed money to. But the takeover fell through, and Montrose Insurance went bust. This chap lost £500 and threatened to kill me if I didn't cover his losses."

Kate huffed.

"So, you came up with a fabricated takeover story for Lady Alsop to swallow."

"Yes, but Eliza overheard us. I tried to explain it to her at the stables, but she threatened to tell Major Tipton..."

"You tried to kill Jane, you rat," said Harry.

"It was nothing personal," said Hammond.

Ridley shook his head.

"Constable, get him out of my sight."

"Yes sir!" responded Constable Roberts prior to hauling Hammond off to a waiting police car.

A few moments later, Ridley called Kate and Jane aside.

"That was remarkable detective work. Thanks."

"A classic swindle," said Kate. "It just took a while for Jane to see the whole picture."

Ridley nodded. "If it weren't for two admirable ladies, he would have got away with it."

Jane smiled. "From both of us, you're welcome."

Forty-Two

A few minutes after the constables had driven Archie Hammond off to Eastbourne, Kate was on the terrace by the library, looking out across the grounds. In the dazzling late sunshine, she took a deep breath and let it out slowly.

Eliza's death had been a shock for all on the Five Oaks estate, but at least Imelda had avoided a nasty fraud. Undoubtedly, Archie Hammond would have fobbed her off with a never-ending series of excuses and broken promises. Few will admit to being conned, especially the likes of Lady Alsop, to whom secrecy around personal finances was absolute. She would have suffered in silence.

Kate took a few steps along the terrace to the open sitting room French doors. The voices inside were those of Chief Inspector Ridley and the doughty Sergeant Nixon, who were both due to depart.

"…in the end, it's up to you, Sergeant. If you'd like to become a detective, you'll need to decide which kind of detective you want to be. There are those who ignore all outside opinions, then there are those, such as me, who consider them. It doesn't make me less of a copper. I trust myself to set aside other opinions if they don't get me anywhere, but why rule out…"

Kate crept farther along the terrace. She hoped the sergeant was listening to Ridley's excellent advice. She would have considered it further, but new voices could be heard in the drawing room through the open French doors.

"Will you marry me?" said Harry.

Had Kate's eyes widened any further she would have risked a strain.

"Yes," said Jane.

Kate was stunned… and delighted.

Actually, she wanted to let out a great 'whoop!' but decided against it. Instead, she made a mental note not to have heard it.

"Let's not wait," said Jane. "How about this summer?"

"But your father—"

"My father will be delighted that we're to be married at all. How does June sound?"

"June? As in three months' time?"

"You haven't changed your mind already, have you?"

"Never. June sounds perfect."

Kate thought how wonderful it was for young people to embrace. For older people it was… exactly the same! The years may have piled up, but her heart still beat in the same way.

She tiptoed away towards the dining room French doors, which too were open. Inside Major Tipton was with Imelda.

"…I feared if I left, Hammond might nip in ahead of me. Although I misread the situation, it's made me realize how deeply I feel."

"I'm glad you stayed, Peter."

"I confided in Lady Jane that I wanted to show my love for you with a gesture. I'll admit my mind was set on buying you the biggest bunch of flowers… but she persuaded me to do something more meaningful – to bring Pippa home."

"Jane advised you to do that?"

"Yes, well, her advice came in two parts. First, get Pippa back."

"And second?"

"Well… Jane *strongly* suggested that I ask you to marry me. I have to say, personally, I think she's spot on with that advice."

Lady Alsop laughed. "So do I, Peter."

"You will then? You'll marry me?"

"Yes, I will."

Kate turned and with eyes dead ahead walked swiftly back to the library French doors, where Perry caught sight of her.

"Kate, look here. I've found a rare and valuable first edition signed by the author."

Kate stepped into the room where Perry handed her a copy of *A Tale of Two Cities* by Charles Dickens.

"Oh my!" she beamed.

Perry pointed to a pile on the table.

"That's sixteen rather good books. Imelda can keep them or sell them. It'll be a tidy sum."

Kate kissed him on the cheek.

"Well done, Perry."

"These others can go to libraries and schools."

He was indicating hundreds of books stacked on the floor beneath Jasper's painting.

"And the books upstairs?" wondered Kate.

"I'll come back next month for a couple of days. I'll soon have it all sorted out."

"Well," said Kate. "I reckon that's everything then."

Perry's frown said otherwise.

"Um… perhaps not everything, Kate. I'm due back at Oxford on Monday."

"Yes, of course."

"Right, so…"

"Is there something else, Perry?"

"Yes, just one other thing… um… Kate, will you marry me?"

"Oh… goodness!"

"I love you, Kate, and I would be the happiest man in England if you would say yes."

"Yes, but…"

"Yes, but…?" Perry looked deflated.

"Another couple has beaten us to it."

"What...? You mean...?"

"Yes, there's another happiest man in England."

"Harry?"

"Yes, well, Major Tipton too, I expect. But I was mainly thinking of Harry."

Perry was beaming. "Jane and Harry. That's wonderful. When did they make the announcement?"

"Ah... they haven't. Not yet."

"Oh?"

"I was near... possibly too near... well, you know how these things go."

"They'll be as surprised and pleased at our news then. A joint announcement!"

Kate wondered about that.

"Perry, they're young and everything's going to be a whirl of excitement, what with family and society gatherings to celebrate the marriage of an earl's daughter. We've both been around the quadrangle before. What say we take a step back and let them have all the congratulations to themselves?"

"Yes... yes, why not... of course. You're absolutely right, Kate. As always! Besides, when it's our turn, I'm sure Jane will want to get involved."

"We can be certain of it – and I'd prefer her to enjoy her own wedding first."

"Yes... so... they'll be looking at next year, perhaps?"

"I think I heard June."

"June next year... yes, that makes sense."

"June *this year.*"

"Oh!"

"We won't have to wait too long for ours."

Perry laughed.

"No, we won't."

"I do love you, Professor Peregrine Nash. I've done so for some time."

"And I think the world of you, Kate. I never thought love would come my way again."

"Right, well… when Jane and Harry tell us their news, remember to look incredibly surprised."

"Yes, of course."

Not for the first time, Kate wondered where she and Perry would live. He was based in Oxford and she in Sandham. But as they went to join Jane and Harry, she set the matter aside. This wasn't the time.

No sooner they met up, Jane had some exciting news.

"Aunt Kate! Professor! We're getting married!"

Kate appeared to be stunned.

"You are?"

"Yes, we are!"

There was nothing false about Kate's heart bursting with joy or the tears now flowing down her cheeks.

"Jane… Harry… that's wonderful!"

"It'll be a June wedding," said Harry.

"June?" said Perry. "That's um…"

"Three months away," said Harry.

"Well, well," said Kate. "That's effective planning. Next, you'll be telling us you've sorted out your honeymoon!"

"We have," said Jane.

"Really? I was joking. Paris?"

"Denmark," said Harry.

"Oh. How interesting."

"You're not kidding," said Jane. "Not so long ago, they found the well-preserved remains of a blonde-haired Bronze Age girl near Egtved. Apparently, she even has neatly trimmed fingernails."

"Oh, that's terrific," said Perry. "I can't think of a better honeymoon!"

"Absolutely," echoed Kate. "I'm sure it beats the Eiffel Tower!"

Forty-Three

So much had been decided in such a short space of time that Kate, alone in the vestibule, was almost dizzy with it all.

In the next few minutes, Jane and Harry would begin the one-hour drive to his parents to share their exciting news. Then tomorrow, they would go to see Jane's father, who was due back after lunch. Of course, Harry was a little nervous. Although Robert would be delighted, he *was* the Earl of Oxley and tradition demanded that Harry seek his permission to marry Jane.

As for Mrs Katherine Forbes and Professor Peregrine Nash? They wouldn't be announcing their own exciting news just yet. They would however be staying overnight at Alsop House – and they were already looking forward to dinner with Imelda and Peter.

And as for Imelda, she had already insisted on presenting Kate with a gift, and Kate had already chosen it: *The Empress of Watering Places, A Brief History of Eastbourne's Seaside, 1752 – 1920.*

As a champion of Sandham-on-Sea's growing reputation, she had a healthy appetite for this kind of book.

Perry, Jane, and Harry came to join her… immediately followed by Chief Inspector Ridley and Sergeant Nixon.

"Great news about Lady Alsop and Major Tipton's wedding plans," said Ridley.

"Absolutely," said Kate, "and they're not the only ones!"

Ridley eyed Kate and the professor, forcing Kate to rapidly redirect him.

"Jane and Harry are to wed!"

"Oh… Oh! Wonderful!"

Jane was beaming.

"You and Mrs Ridley are invited."

"Oh, thanks very much! That's lovely!"

Jane gave him a big hug, which, judging by his look of sheer surprise and delight, was a rare way for Chief Inspector Ridley of Scotland Yard to finish off an important case.

A few moments later, Major Tipton and Lady Alsop, hand in hand, led everyone out to the front of the house, where the cars were waiting.

Kate smiled. Major Tipton was definitely the right man for Lady Alsop.

Immediately, there was much praise for the staff, who had worked hard under difficult circumstances. Then Kate

257

spotted Brian Webster and Billy the stable boy standing a little way off. Major Tipton had already promised that the stables would be restored to their former glory. Imelda was even planning to resume riding again. As for the Alsop Challenge Cup, it would be held later in the year and then every year. Regarding that, Kate and Jane had asked that their stake money be allocated to the staff alongside Lady Alsop's to give Mr Brooke, Connie, George, and Cook three chances of winning next time rather than one.

Kate approached Brian and Billy.

"It seems the stables are to have a new lease of life," she said. "I hope that makes things easier for you."

"It does," said Brian. "There's no other place I'd rather be."

Billy grinned. "Same for me, Ma'am. And we're to get another stable boy, who'll I'll train to be a good 'un."

"Wonderful," said Kate, passing Billy a few silver coins. "Best of luck."

Kate turned back to the house where the first preparing to leave were Jonathan Deerhurst and Sophie Pearce who were heading back to London. They would be dropping Miss Glessing off home on the way. At the same time, Dr Evans emerged from the house with Jasper.

"No hard feelings?" said Ridley to the younger man.

"No, but I'm glad I had Mrs Forbes and Lady Jane on my side!"

Ridley agreed then made a point of thanking the doctor for having the courage to do the right thing.

"It was tough for you, but you came around to putting Justice first. If there's ever another serious crime down this way, I know I can count on you."

The doctor's eyes were moist.

"Thank you, Chief Inspector. I'll never let you down."

The doctor then thanked Kate and Jane before getting into his car with Jasper.

Kate smiled at Ridley.

"What a lovely man you are, Chief Inspector."

All waved off Jonathan's car and were about to do the same for Dr Evans… when David Marston came running out of the house, a bag in one hand, the other waving frantically.

"Wait for me!"

Kate laughed as he scrambled onto the back seat of the doctor's car with as much dignity as a circus clown.

Sergeant Nixon then thanked Kate and Jane for their help before getting into the remaining police car with the chief inspector.

All waved as they pulled away.

Now it was time to see off Jane and Harry with big hugs and lots of love.

Into her mid-fifties, life for Kate Forbes continued to move in the unexpected direction it had taken on teaming up with her niece. Having feared becoming lonely and insignificant, Kate had embraced so much. There was still much to be resolved of course, but it was a future full of promise. Top of the immediate list was Jane and Harry's wedding. Then her own. One, a grand affair befitting the daughter of an earl, the other a more low-key event in Sandham-on-Sea... or Oxford.

Well, that would be decided in due course.

Waving Jane and Harry's car off, Kate reached for Perry's hand, which he took.

"Things seem to have turned out quite well," she said.

Perry smiled warmly. "I've never seen Jane and Harry look happier. Come to think of it, I've never seen us look happier either!"

Kate laughed – and as they squeezed hands, she knew this really was a new chapter... and that there was so much more of the story to come.

THE END (Until Next Time...)

Thank you for reading **Murder at Five Oaks Stables**

If you enjoyed it, why not leave a review on Amazon. It's a great way to encourage others to take a chance on Aunt Kate and Lady Jane's adventures.

Don't miss the next book in the series:

"The Winthrop Castle Affair"

For details of all books by B. D. Churston, please visit our website.

www.churstonmysteries.com

Printed in Great Britain
by Amazon

61924761R00152